LAUGHING IN THE SHADOW OF BULLETS

LAUGHING IN THE SHADOW OF BULLETS

Sunita Bali

Ocean Books Pvt. Ltd.
ISO 9001:2008 Publishers

Published by
Ocean Books (P) Ltd.
4/19 Asaf Ali Road,
New Delhi-110 002 (INDIA)
e-mail: info@oceanbooks.in

ISBN 978-81-8430-189-2

Laughing in the Shadow of Bullets
by Sunita Bali

Edition
First, 2013

Price
Rs. 200.00 (Rs. Two Hundred only)

Printed at
Bhanu Printers, Delhi

Dedicated to:

1. Papa (Late Shri J.C. Vaid),
without whom I could not have
got my Military moorings.

2. Pragati, my daughter, who suggested
and encouraged this book.

3. The never-yielding spirit of Indian
Combat Soldiering.

Concept Inception

"Laugh and be merry.
Remember better the world with a song.
Better the world with a blow in the teeth of a wrong.
Laugh and be merry.
Together like brothers akin.
Guesting a while in the rooms of a beautiful inn."

–John Masefield

Even if the girls were permitted to join the service when I was in the eligible age, I would never have ventured. Actually, girls were always a part of the service albeit specially in the Army Medical Corps (AMC) as doctors and in the Military Nursing Services (MNS) as nurses but those were never my cup of tea-coffee.

After my marriage to a military officer, I became a part of the Army. More than three decades of this association, or should I say in cricketing terms this 'Unbeaten Partnership', gave me both a Grand Stand as also a Close Quarter view of the Military life. I have since been coloured Olive Green (OG) totally and have even picked up their language.

My complete OG transformation is like the good old English teacher, who was locked along with a young Natha Singh to teach him English but emerged from his dual confinement of a protracted period lamenting in chaste Punjabi, "Natha nahi sikh sakda" (Natha cannot learn).

During these long years, I have seen these strange men laugh, joke and enjoy together even in the midst of most trying conditions. After my husband's super annuation while with my daughter, Pragati in UK, she suggested to me that I articulate my experiences of Army from my point of view in black and white.

Since the Indian Official Secret Act never permitted me to be privy to serious military matters, I present my experiences as an extended version of 'Humour in Uniform', with a few exceptions, wherein I found myself obliged to convey certain other aspects of soldiering. This volume is, therefore, a collation of various incidents that I saw or heard, first or second hand and may afford a rare view to those who have not been lucky enough to see this peculiar and great organization from effective range. To those lucky ones who have been integral to it, I present a nostalgic recollection.

Before I proceed further as a non-essential safety catch, I wish to request my readers not to get away with the concept that the Army is all fun, frolic and laugh. While it surely is all these, but is in actuality much more. It is a serious profession of Arms where actual bullets and bombs fly and where death and blood are integral to life.

With due respect to the present day Management Gurus from the best of universities, I would like to submit that while their target at the end of the day is better output and improved productivity, the Army leadership motivates their men to give their blood, limbs and life for the cause, in the face of sure danger, and then the infantry, certainly the only organization, where men go to kill or die only on verbal orders. Be it a Colonel-Commanding Officer (CO) or a Naik (Section Commander), no subordinate questions his judgement and none demands anything in writing. They hear his verbal orders, make their notes, if required, and rush to sacrifice their lives for a small non-descript hill, a sand dune, a river bed or a piece of bare land, which they might not have ever seen and may never see it again. Disobedience to such lawful command is a very serious offence under the Army Act and is more severely punishable if committed in the face of the enemy attack.

My self-imposed mandate or the term of reference, as the soldiers would call it, in this book is not to indulge in serious military matters for I frankly lack the locus standi. I, therefore, will only invest in the lighter side of this very serious profession.

The anecdotes you will read and perhaps enjoy are part fictitious and part real with a certain colouring of my imagination for whatever worth that be, because I certainly have no claims to the lineage of William Wordsworth or his equally worthy friend, Colridge. I am, however, attempting a set of 'Spectator's Papers' knowing fully well that had Addison or Steele been alive, I would have been sued in the court of ethics if not law, but then some amount of bravado I too have acquired.

Through these pages, I wish to place my thanks to all those men and women whom I have named and who have, through their unique acts, inspired me to write this book. I also write *ab-initio* apologise to all those considerate Gentlemen and Ladies, who feel, after going through these lines that I have, due to my own inadequacy of expression or information, been less than fair to them.

Happy reading then and let us laugh together for that is becoming increasingly rare in the contemporary lifestyle. I also request to invoke the much talked about 'Willing Suspension of Disbelief' from my readers to fully savour the intended fun.

Contents

1

Mismatch in Waterloo

"A woman lost her husband. When the funeral journey had just about begun, the bier accidently struck against a tree. The impact miraculously revived the man. He got up and lived for another five to six years and then re-died. This time when the pall bearers were about to take him out *de novo*, the woman spontaneously asked them to be careful of the tree" – and then they say marriages are made in heavens and are only formalised on earth. Well, mine was not that long distance affair, for it was made in Agra (we all know Agra is not only famous for Mughal architecture but is also known for some not very complimentary aspects) and formalised just about 200 km away in Delhi.

Strangely, but surely, I was never infatuated by uniform of any kind – Army, Navy, Air Force or, for that matter, any other central service. I had successfully avoided even the NCC, which was mandatory during my college days.

My father, a Banker by profession had diagonally opposite views. He thought very little of the 'bloody civilians' apart from his own self and, perhaps, a very selected caucus around him. He interacted with senior Army officers; he socialised with them and, in fact, even lived like them. Surprisingly, however, he never regretted not having joined the Army and, more surprisingly, always lamented his not becoming a Vet Surgeon.

When me and my elder sister Neelam grew up, my mother started compelling my fathr for finding suitable matches.

When my elder sister, Neelam and me, two years her junior, were coming of age, our mother, like all wives, started making her husband's life anything but bed of roses and compelled him to start. Our 'civilian' but totally 'non-civilian' father concentrated his search exclusively among the Army officers and, before long, succeeded in finding Major Kapil Dutt, an infantry officer, for my elder sister. The whole family was surprised.

They say an inkling should be enough for a wise person. Here for me the writing was on the wall but then as Lord Byron said, "Why delay the truth, and eventually the inevitable happened. Major VK Bali from the SIKH LIGHT INFANTRY (SIKH LI) was my Waterloo. Another coup of the sort was completed by destiny. I, a totally dedicated academician, a Gold Medalist with an extraordinar record in M.Sc. (Zoology) and he, who by his own admission, albeit exaggerated, hardly cleared a class in one year. He tried to impress me with his science knowledge by showcasing what was imparted to him as 'Science and Warfare' during his Pre-commissioned Training in Officers' Training Academy (OTA) Chennai. His scientific knowledge was of Muzzle Velocity, Nuclear Blast, Rockets, Missiles and Troposcatter Communications and more such subjects, and when he learnt that I had studied and studied well Biology upto B.Sc., he spoke about the first-aid pamphlet that he had read to pass his 'Part B' and 'Part C' promotion examinations. Well, the fact is that the mismatch was complete and sealed and we took off on the journey of life, unmindful of the anomalies of our back and foreground.

Right in the initial phase of our joint steps, he suggested that whoever made lesser money per month, should quit job and join the richer partner and I became disappointed to discover that a Major's emoluments were more than that of a lecturer. I unwillingly resigned to be with him. Overtly to this date he cherishes it as the only victory against me as if I came from the other side of the LoC (Line of Control).

The next major issue that required deliberate handling was the selection of the location for the Honeymoon, and the financial status for the sustenance of the period. It is pertinent to mention here that our marriage was without any give and take of money or dowry for the square peg that I had got was an idealistic character too. Well, the richer of two of us that was he, had Rs. 9,500/- after eight years of service and that too in the Defence Services Officer's Provident Fund (DSOP), which he could not withdraw. I, from my one-and-a-half years of college teaching, had Rs. 4,000/- in my tight control. Besides, we also had the supreme luxury of having his monthly pay for that month, which was much this side of the four figures.

For the grand trip, he would not even think of the Himalayas for those only reminded him of his Operational Areas. Western Ghats and Vindhyachal likewise reminded him of his training days and were considered to be inadequate and inappropriate. Considering the money we had, Nilgiris were like going abroad, thus, the process of elimination led us to the Satpuras and we homed on to its only hill station—Panchmarhi. The proximity of our intended destination and its friendly impact on our joint purse were also clinching arguments.

When the journey was about to commence from New Delhi Railway Station, a distant uncle of mine with genuine concern inquired as to when would we be back and without giving it a thought, our spontaneous response was that it all was to be guided by the longevity of our pooled financial resources.

The Punjab Mail look us to our Rail Head and from there we reached Panchmarhi by road with all the difficulties.

❑

2

Neither Honey Nor Moon

> *"Smile and the world smiles with you and laugh when the world laughs at you."*
>
> **—Anonymous**

Panchmarhi is a small hill station with small height in the second biggest state of the country, which, at that time, was the biggest (MP). Chattisgarh had not yet been formed.

Approximately, two hours of road journey from the rail head, Pipariya, and both of us, for the first time in our lives, were greeted by female porters. Chivalry in him was, and continued to be, brimming and we, thus, had to carry our own luggage and we all knew those were not the days of wheelers. Quite well exhausted, I reached our hotel. The young bride in me had never visualised such a beginning to such a sojourn. Logically after a quick dinner, we both fell asleep like logs.

Next morning was bright, late and comfortable and we had decided to laze and saunter around but by forenoon, we were adequately reposed and were yearning to be back to activity. A tourist map of the area was painted on the walls of the hotel lobby. I was and I continue to be addicted to read everything that is written or printed or painted around me. I identified all the tourist spots of the town and of the area of interest around it. We both selected a waterfall, some 10 to 12 km away from the town, deep in the jungle, as our maiden trek.

The Hotel Manager offered to arrange a guide but for a prohibitive sum of Rs. 10/-. This was unthinkably insulting for an infantry soldier, who, as he said, was better trained to handle a jungle trek than all the 'bloody civilians' of Panchmarhi put together. He, with an imperious disdain, took a paper and a pen and drew a weird sketch, which he called as a 'Navigational Chart', on it and was quite confident of making it a successful trip on the strength of that strange and funny looking drawing. Being good at Botany and Zoology, I too was exceedingly proud of my sketching. I independently made a sketch of our likely area of operations. Having thus armed ourselves, we took off after lunch by about 2 O'clock in the afternoon.

By the time we had our first glimpse of the fall, it was about 4 O'clock in the evening and the sky was already overcast. We quite admired the water falling down but did not rest only with that. We decided to reach the very spot where the water was falling and commenced our 'Advance to Contact'. Another half an-hour's move through the jungle, which was becoming increasingly dense, both of us could make out that by the time we would reach and turn back, it would be dark and raining. Both of us, however, did not want to compromise our fears and perhaps wanted to impress each other. But I blinked first and little later suggested an 'About Turn'. It was certainly not acceptable to his soldierly/infantry pride and we continued and, at last, did reach our intended spot, where the huge fall was 'linking up' with ground. But then, as expected, the higher waterfall from the clouds too had begun and the 'last light' of the day was just around. Both of us were quite apprehensive of the situation we were in, for both of us had independently noticed that throughout our jungle walk, we had not encountered any human form. Actually, the only living being that we saw was an abandoned cow, but this lament of ours was immediately taken care of by the God of the Woods and a huge team of wild apes of all colours and sizes appeared from nowhere. Our eye for natural beauty had been long lost and now it appeared to be an unequal battle of survival.

Making loud, wild nerve-shattering sounds, they gathered all around us but without paying us any attention. We withdrew into the pool as deep as we could upto the depth of our nostrils and they had fully enveloped us both vertically from the tree tops as also horizontally from the water edge. Somehow they were perhaps not thirsty and were also not in a regatta mood. Hanumanji had very kindly kept his Army in the good humour. They perhaps had a good and sumptuous meal and were least interested in us. Having enjoyed themselves at our cost and imposing another about half-an-hour's delay on us, they 'retreated' but that was only the beginning of our troubles.

A few minutes into our return trail and it was pretty dark and pouring quite heavily and the 'Moon' was badly and irretrievably clouded. We had, of course, no access to the 'Honey' and even if we had, its utility was nix. Wet, tired and hungry, we had by then lost not only the 'Honey' and 'Moon' but also our route. Our Navigation charts got clean washed and had 'vanished' beyond usefulness. We did not even know 'Own Position', the 'Start Point' for any worthwhile navigation and could make nothing of where we were heading. Fighting and comforting each other, we kept moving, now well into night and jungle. He kept telling me that walking is no great deal, you just need to move your rear foot in front of the one ahead. It did not impress me then and it does not impress me now. Walking certainly can be very tedious and each foot gathers immoveable weight, and, of course, it was so at that night.

Another thing he always quotes and this I agree with him that 'God looks after fools and infantrymen'. He claims to have his right in both the queues (of fools and infantrymen) and much that I would like to disagree, I find his assessment right.

The first glimmer of hope dawned in the middle of the night, when we again came across the abandoned cow. Much later floundering from one boulder to another, God eventually took pity on us and we found ourselves next to a wall. We quickly analysed that the wall has to have a gate and perhaps someone living inside. Our assessment eventually proved to be half right and half wrong. We jumped inside the wall hoping to find a shelter and help. We must have moved a few steps when a sable cloud from above turned forth its silver lining but not to our advantage, for we discovered ourselves to be in the middle of a graveyard. We were wet, we were tired, we were hungry and now we were also scared—any hope of finding a shelter had vanished, for people around us had long back ceased to exist.

The first spontaneous action in that ghastly situation was to run and get away but we checked ourselves. Had we obeyed our reflexes, we surely would have slipped or hit against a grave stone and fallen and perhaps into the one freshly dug awaiting its guest next morning. Under that contingency, a couple of ghosts or witches or both would certainly have appeared, but we held on, recollected whatever reserves of energy and composure we could and we very deliberately took our steps and reached the gate as expected, but as not expected and as should have been expected, we found it locked. We once again mustered our deepest reserves of energy and courage and climbed out of it and once again as appreciated, were on a road head. As we set our feet on the most beautiful road I have ever seen, we both instinctively started running.

Some distance away a few good men were sitting around a bonfire, perhaps guarding their crop from the wild animals. The road directed us to be running in their direction and if anybody could time that run of ours, we could have put 'Usain Bolt' and his world record to shame, but no those good men were even faster. They shrieked collectively and instead of extending a helping hand, disappeared into their fields. We never realised when and where they melted away and neither did we care. Now, of course, we understand their speed and predicament for they were being attacked by a Ghost and a Witch, who had in front of their eyes, climbed out of the gate of the graveyard.

Much later at about 2 O'clock at night, we reached the cosy comfort of our apartment. We were both tired, wet, hungry, scared and totally exhausted, and to cap it all, I was running a very high fever.

Rest of the Honeymooning was spent in the safe and comforting environs of a Military Hospital, luckily there was one in that station, but we did save some good money, and that was my honey moon.

❑

3

A Young Initiative

"A young girl and her grandmother were sitting on their terrace while her father was working in the lawn down below. The old lady was doing some needle work and the girl was just looking around, when she spotted a body of troops advancing towards them from a distance. She told her grandma that some soldiers were advancing towards them. The old lady instructed her to get in immediately and the girl reluctantly obeyed. However, from inside the room, she kept watching the advancing soldiers, who, by that time had come nearer and she could now see them wearing turbans and she accordingly announced the latest discovery to the wise old owl, who told the young lady to keep the door open and herself also moved in. Having moved in, the old lady got busy but the young girl kept surveying the scene. She now announced to her grandmother that the soldiers were wearing SIKH LI on their shoulders. The old lady immediately asked her son also to move in. That is SIKH LI *albeit* in a lighter vein, otherwise an excellent group of combat troops, full of *josh* and initiative with many a famous victories to their credit. This is the regiment to which Vijay (Vj) belongs and that is where I joined him.

This was the time when war clouds were already gathering on the horizon. Situation was tense, to say the least, and everybody knew it could be any-time. Family visits were stopped, and those who were there, were asked to leave. I was there with him for a few days and had already booked my return journey, which was to commence a few days later.

The house in which we stayed was lavish. An iron sheet (CGI) door provided the privacy. A smaller tent pitched behind was our bathroom, which contained a reversed rum box and a half cut ghee tin from the empty stock of the unit canteen as the toilet, but situation was excellent and we enjoyed a great deal.

Vj was doing Adjutant of the unit as he most of the time did and had to be available to his boss, the Commanding Officer (CO) 24 × 7 as also to the rest of the unit, a body of approximately 1000 men as his constant link. He had a few telephones which were robust enough to break stones if thus utilised and there were equal number of radio sets, which the non-military readers will understand as wireless. All of them had the habit of being constantly vocal irrespective of the appropriateness of the time. Mercifully the mobile phones had not yet arrived on the scenes. There were a couple of men posted round the clock to man all those communication devices and kept calling Vj invariably, frantically and with urgency.

The unit was, as they used to call in an eyeball to eyeball confrontation on the Cease Fire Line (CFL), the term Line of Control (LoC) was a later substitute. Logically, as expected the post nearest to the enemy was being commanded by 2/ Lt. Ajay, a young officer in his early twenties, full of enthusiasm and initiative. His Company Commander, a Major in his thirties, was away for some reason and the responsibility of commanding the company of approximately 150 men was on his young and willing shoulders.

Beyond the middle of the night, there was a knock at the door and a radio set was brought in, for the young man spoken above had something hot to convey to the Adjutant. The conversation that took place on the radio set was in a very hushed tone and low volume but I have always prided over my audio capabilities. I recount the dialogue as it went to the best of my memory, which again is one of my very few assets.

(a) Hello Charlie One, message over.
(b) Charlie One OK, over.
(c)Struck across the line, over.
(d) Across, what the hell are you doing there?, over.
(e) Patrolling, over.
(f) Who ordered this patrol, who sent you?, over.
(g) No one, only my initiative, over.
(h) How far are you from them?, over.
(i) Enemy post approximately 300 meters behind, over.
(j) Rush back immediately, over.
(k) Cannnot enemy patrol right opposite, over.
(l) Shit, how far?, over.
(m) Not sure, perhaps 100 meters, over.
(n) And you are in their territory, over.
(o) Yes, but their patrol is in our territory?, over.
(p) Why the hell you went there?, over.
(q) Wanted to put the Indian flag on their post, over.
(r) Who gave you this flag?, over.
(s) We made it ourselves and have already planted it there.

Cannot talk anymore, they are closing in, over.

Next hour and a half were very tense and then again the young flag-bearer came up but this time on telephone.

(a) Hello Sir, Good Morning, we are back and safe.

(b) I do not know whether the morning is going to be good for you. You may be back but are not yet safe. The Old Man (CO is often called Old Man in the unit) will like to see you well and proper first thing in the morning.

(c) Right Sir, I will be there.

(d) No, you better start immediately to be in time and I hope all the men and equipment you so idiotically took along are safe and fine.

(e) Yes Sir.

(f) Okay then, see you.

I am not privy to whatever transpired in the hot office in the cold unpleasant morning but I know that the young man survived and survived to rise upto the rank of a Brigadier. He was, thereafter, called 2/Lt. Initiative in the unit by the other officers and he himself too enjoyed his new nomenclature. And people talk of zero mistake syndrome!

❑

4

The Battle Inoculation

"A smile is most needed when confronted with sure danger."
– Anonymous

The war was slowly and gradually closing in. Vijay (Vj), as he has always been spelling his name) was tasked to protect an Air Force unit from likely para drop. He had taken up his position around the Vulnerable Area (VA) and had his underground Command Post (CP) also constructed there. He used to be available there round the clock alongwith his men. Very early in the morning before the first light "Stand To" or morning alert, he used to come to the room allotted to him in the Air Force Officers' Mess to get ready and be back.

Slightly away from his position around the VA, Air Defence (AD) Guns were deployed to protect the same VA from enemy air raid. Coincidently, the officer in command of the AD was a childhood friend of Vj and was also his course mate from the OTA. One had to see both of them to realise the art of having fun and great time even in those extreme intense times. They both shared that room to get ready in the morning and since both of them had to get back in the same timeframe, there was always a scramble to get ready.

It was during this time that I got an opportunity to visit him for a couple of days. I was quite surprised and amused that the two friends compelled by the demand of punctuality had resorted to an open bathroom just like the open kitchens of modern times. There were no bolts and the access was free, which allowed both of them to get ready simultaneously.

On one such night after dinner (this is a second hand account as Vj subsequently narrated to me) when he was about to settle down at his CP after going around his defence, he got a telephone call from his friend inviting him for a late night pudding. Vj and most of his friends do not have a sweet-tooth but have what I call 'Sweet 32' (By now, of course, in 2012, those 32 must be in 20s if not in teens). Such invitations are never refused and both the friends were soon sharing the ample quantity of kheer alongwith their childhood memories when suddenly the sky above opened up. This to date is the only time when Vj abandoned his pudding. Both of them rushed out, ran to their respective CPs. Since Vj was guesting it was a longer run, perhaps of approximately 600 meters for him. The sky was red, resounding and unnerving. As per Vj, he had never felt so alone. Fear is a natural reaction but the success lies in controlling and overcoming it. The first reaction of the 'Solitary Reaper' running to regain his CP, was to immediately go to ground in the available natural folds, but then the soldier in him took over, he got up and moving briskly under the bombs and rockets released by the enemy aircraft reached his men to take control. He calls it as his final battle inoculation, which subsequently never failed him.

❑

5

My Maiden Visit Abroad

"A smile costs less than electricity but reflects more light."

– Anonymous

A quick redeployment and they were once again moved to eyeball to eyeball confrontation. Next few days for us, who were in the cosy comforts of our houses, were very anxious. There was little known about him or his unit but for the fact that they were in the Western Theatre.

The biggest calming factor was Vj's father, Bauji, himself a retired soldier. He never showed any anxiety inspite of having three of his four sons in uniform, facing the enemy at different locations. My civilian and yet 'noncivilian' father was no less in his composure and eventually it all rubbed on us too.

The biggest post second world war victory happened. Round about one lakh Pakistani soldiers surrendered to the Indian Army alongwith their weapons. India was a very proud nation and we were lucky to be around that time. Only if the present electronic media coverage was available at that time, but this justifiable regret is now in retrospect, at that time whatever was available was adequate and India was actually and truly shining.

From somewhere one day, he spoke on telephone and things started to fall in place and life started its recourse to normalcy. Some time later, the families were permitted to meet their men folk for a short period.

I reached his unit but that night could only speak to him on those field telephones which, if used offensively, could even be lethal. Next morning, I started rather early to meet him and it was quite a frantic feeling when we crossed the International Border, without Passport, without Visa and without any security check in a truck One Ton. Sitting behind, I enjoyed my maiden visit abroad, tossing like a ball on seats made most comfortable by spreading a black hardy Army blanket, fully covered by the dust that was being kicked up. Mercifully, the flight to the foreign land was not very long and I survived. I would not be very confident if I would be able to sustain a repeat performance today without slipping a spinal disc—yes women too age.

We were treated to a sumptuous lunch and all possible 'pakoras' even of some wild grass and, thereafter, some nice Punjabi and Hindi songs.

One of Vj's men with an earthy-village sense of humour, had kept a small stray dog as his pet. He had very wittingly given the little pup a famous name from across the line which was running along a river. The little pup used to bark at the bigger dogs and his wise master would instantaneously warn him to learn from the blunders of the other side, who by barking at the bigger neighbour had ended up losing half of their own.

This pup was not the only pet of the post. They had also kept a goat, which was received in rations as Meat on Hoaf (MOH) but had somehow survived because of the affection of the Ration NCO (Non-Commissioned Officer). He was given an Indian name, Nalha Singh and was surprisingly well disciplined. He would be standing in line for PT and would also go around through the communication trenches at the time of first and last light stand to.

❑

6

Local Liaisons

"Whoever delights in solitude is either a wild beast or an angel."

– Francis Bacon

Soldiers can have no such claims. Peace had finally returned and we were living comfortably there with the locals. Army's stock with the general public was at its best, having brought the biggest glory of the recent times to the country. The locals were more than friendly and some of the best accomodations of the villages in that area were willingly made available to the unit. Everyone, however, was not that lucky as some of us continued to dwell in the abandoned Railway buildings, whose demolition was stayed to be of use to us. Some others were in tentage and most single officers and men continued to be in the bunkers. No one, however, grudged anyone and it was like an extended, not only joint but cohesive, family.

In such blissful but still tense situation, after the war had just ended and we were still in effective range, the enemy too was smarting under the most humiliating defeat, which perhaps is still the case. Some romantic local liaisons were quite a spontaneous consequence. One of the men got married to a local girl and even got its due recognition and coverage. Somehow none of the officers went that far ahead.

Bholi was a local woman and lived a 21st Century USA lifestyle. Two of the men of the unit in their leisure had left some important item at her residence. The lost item was discovered in the routine evening count and some quick and timely action got it recovered from Bholi's residence. The guilty twosome were caught and were administered a sound blanket treatment as they had rightfully deserved.

Having suffered the lavish treatment under the blankets, the two erring men were moaning and sighing endlessly on the floor, 'Hai Bholi, Hai Bholi' and shifting the blame to each other while expressing their individual innocence. Thence onward, 'Hai Bholi' became a mock cry of the unit officers whenever they were tired or in pain and it continues even today inspite of good about three generations of officers having changed. In fact, I was quite amused to know that some of the children of the officers have also taken to this 'Crying' without even knowing the history and geography of its inception. Where good old Bholi is now is not known but she is immortalised in the hearts of these men, many of whom have never even seen her. That is loyalty—for you.

❑

7

An International/Inter-service Cooperation

"The first quality in a soldier is constancy in enduring fatigue and hardship."

–Napoleon

On an fateful day, we were invited by a forward company commander to a Pakistani lunch, which we all attended and enjoyed. Later, we learnt that it was prepared by a Pakistani cook, who had come from across the line. To date, no one has explained the presence of that man in our cook house to me, whether he was a Prisoner of War (PoW), or had strayed across or was trying to escape for being a Bengali, but that notwithstanding, he was an excellent cook.

This lunch was also attended by a couple of Air Force Officers. It was an interesting afternoon, which indeed became historical due to the incident narrated in the succeeding paragraphs.

A discussion on physical fitness ensued at the time of having pudding and it zeroed on to the fact that who could do maximum sit ups. Most of the officers confessed to a capability of 30 to 50 till the query reached Major Bhupal Chandra, a very mild mannered and soft-spoken toughie. Chandra batted his eyelids and surprised everyone by stating that at a stretch at any one time, he could do 1,000 sit ups.

I, for one, did not even know what the hell a sit up was, but most of the people, who knew about it, attributed the unimaginable quote of 1,000 to the height Major Chandra must have acquired consequent to the couple of bottles of beer that he had till then downed. Major Chauhan, his immediate senior, for some reasons took an exception to this tall talk and dared the man to a bet, which was finalised at 40 bottles of beer. Chandra said that there was no need to fix another time and place. He removed his belt and, there in front of everyone went on the floor.

The two Air Force officers were designated as umpires to watch and all of us rearranged our chairs into a grand stand. The young man, after having had a couple of bottles of beer and after having consumed a good lunch, commenced his pursuit of 1,000 sit ups which everyone knew to be a tall talk. No one was willing to concede a figure of 50s. It, however, did not end there and continued and continued for the next one hour and fifty minutes. He was sweating, was bruised and was bleeding when the two umpires announced that the unthinkable had been achieved. Chandra did another 10 as a safeguard against any miscalculations.

Thereafter, for about two months, he enjoyed his 40 bottles of beer, which of course, no one grudged him. This epitome of physical fitness was later deputed by the CO to head the joint border survey with the Pakistanis, who insisted on his substitution for his relentless move without stopping even for a while. Their request came through the higher HQ and had to be accommodated.

During the war, which had just concluded, the spirited toughie had announced a reward of one bottle of whisky from his side for any Air Force officer returning after destroying an enemy aircraft. He had also expressed a desire to go to see a movie that side of the line, of course such like permissions are never forthcoming.

The time and age have taken a toll on all of us but I hope the gentle toughie is still strong. Our host is, of course, no more and may God grant peace to his soul!

❑

8

Dogs are not Only Loyal, are Vindictive too

There was a huge funeral procession and a dog too was seen accompanying it. In the procession, the gender ratio was heavily in favour of the women. A passerby woman surprisingly asked one of the mourners as to who had passed away. She was taken to the widow of deceased. She approached her and offered her condolences, which were not exactly needed. Then she inquired from the widow the cause of the death and was informed that it was due to the bite of the dog which was also a part of the funeral. The woman looked around and asked her whisperingly if she could borrow the dog for a day. The widow non-chalantly asked her to join the queue of the women, who were following the bier.

Dogs indeed have multifarous usage for mankind but not the one that leads this episode. Major Basith was a gentleman, recognized for his behavioural propriety and soldierly qualities. He was particularly close to Vj. He subsequently shifted to the Indian Police Service (IPS) and retired as the Director General (DG) of Andhra Pradesh.

He and Vj used to share a tent but had the supreme luxury of separate bath-tents (not rooms). One day, while bathing, an impish child, son of Major Grewal, ran away with Major Basith's bath curtain, exposing his well-lathered six packs to involuntary exposure. That was indeed to be a special day for the reluctant bathing beauty. At the end of an embarrassing exposure when Major Basith was sleeping on his bed at night in his tent, a dog infiltrated his tent and mounted up his bed and eventually his chest. When the four-legged beauty was on his chest, I cannot be sure if he/she had four or two legs on him but the weight must have been too much for him to continue his slumber. He opened his eyes and imagine his plight to see a dog next to his nose, but instead of the dog barking, it was the man who took over and barked at the dog and the dog as non-plused as his host withdrew instantaneously.

4. The other occupant of the tent, Vj, thanking his stars to have escaped the lead role in the story, walked out of their lavish lodgings and let the sentry and the Guard Commander have his piece of mind, knowing fully well that such intrusions are truly beyond any control and that too when not suspected.

The morning scene after PT (Physical Training) was still more amusing. The Battalian Havaldar Major (BHM) had rounded up all the dogs of the area and wanted Major Basith to identify the nocturnal intruder.

The matter did end but not exactly there. The 'Dog Squad' did not take kindly to the public insult and within that week itself, took their revenge by biting Major Basith during one of his unsuspecting walks. One could, however, never be sure if it was the same four-legged beauty or some other loyal associate of his. But this time, it ended with the hospitalization of the wounded, nay the bitten soldier and 14 pricks in the belly. Thereafter, it was Cease Fire between the two and the four-legged beings.

❑

9

No Laughing Matter : Whither is the Zero Mistake Syndrome

"When going gets tough, tough gets going."

—Napoleon

The quote is relevant both physically and mentally. Our unit had moved to a proper peace station and we all savoured its facilities for the first time. This tenure, therefore, has the maximum number of incidents, which include both the funniest and the grimmest and I begin with the second category.

The CO was Lt Col AS Sisodia, who Vj regards as his mentor and perhaps does not hold anybody at that level. Truly a soldier of grit, determination and a leader, who inspired everything positive including the bar/bottle hits. The CO is all in all for approximately 1,000 men under him and their families. He is the 'Ma Baap' and is also conversely responsible for all their acts of commission or omission both positive and negative. So far as the families go, the responsibility is also shared by CO's wife, semi-officially. Adjutant is CO's right hand man and does most of the things on his behalf and, thus, many bucks stop at him. Second-in-Command (2IC) of the unit, as the name suggests, is the Number 2 of the unit. He officiates for the CO during his absence and is primarily responsible for the security welfare and accounts. Major Grewal, another gentleman. Vj holds in great esteem was the 2IC and Vj as always was the

Adjutant. There is a popular story about the CO, his Adjutant and the SIKH LI, which must be recounted.

Older SIKH LI COs never considered articulation of Queen's language as a soldierly quality and for them physical fitness was the only requirement. They generally looked for one officer from the 20 they were authorised, who knew the language fairly well and then appointed him as Adjutant who did all their writing work and there is no dearth of that. At the end of the year the CO initiates an Annual Confidential Report (ACR) on all his officers and grades them on a scale of '0 to 9' in various attributes, which include among others Physical Fitness and Expression. When it came to initiating the ACR of the Adjutant, the CO gave him '3' points in Expression. The youngman was justifiably rattled and he went back to the Old Man. He protested that inspite of having written all the communication of the unit, why was he being given a lowly '3' in Expression. The CO very candidly told him because he was not physically fit enough. The youngman did not comprehend the logic which the CO explained. Since expression is not important for SIKH LI officers, he has been given a '3' there and since physical fitness is most important, he has been given a '9' inspite of not being adequately fit. A quid pro quid.

Everything in the unit was going normal. The 2IC had gone on a longish course and Major Alexander was officiating for him. This was the time when the unit was ordered to collect a prisoner from another unit located in the central part of the country. The prisoner was to be kept in the unit Quarter Guard (A mini jail with all the major units of the Army, where men are kept and punished for all the offences under the Army Act) and was to be produced for interrogation as and when required.

SIKH LI Quarter Guards (QG) are generally well populated. Addition of one more prisoner was no great issue and the orders were being complied with. During this time, the CO went for one day's leave and Major Alexander took over the unit *albeit* for one day. For an active soldier as said above, CO is a big thing and taking over the unit is equally momentous, but certainly not for such like short periods.

More as fun and frolic, all the officers got around Major Alex and his wife and demanded a party from them. Loveable couple that they are, they too joined in and a dinner was organized at their place. We were all there till well past midnight, which in itself was a departure from the set norms of the otherwise very sober and disciplined unit.

It was summer time and we were sleeping outside when, at about 4 am, the QG bell sounded alarm. It was only at a distance of about 300 meters from our place. Immediately, the whole unit gathered there and it transpired that the prisoner, who was brought from the other unit, had escaped.

Hell was let loose and it was then that the unit realised that the escapee was a serious security threat. Immediately, a cordon of about 3 km radius was established around the unit. The escape was reported to the higher HQ.

By about 10 am, a Court of Inquiry (C of I) headed by a Brigadier, a very senior officer was convened and was ordered to find out the reason within 72 hours. The investigations began sooner than expected.

At about 12 'o'clock, the CO arrived back from his one day's leave and was co-incidently running with high temperature. The 2IC, Adjutant and the Subedar Major (SM) went to receive him. He was getting down from his vehicle when he saw the trio approaching. He remarked that all three of them coming together meant there was something drastically wrong. He was apprised of the incident. He looked at Vj and said, "Vj, you have let me down," and that was the only rebuke Vj received in his entire career, and that too from a man, who was otherwise famous for his sorting out of errant men well and proper. The CO walked in and asked Vj to meet him after some time.

As ordered, the Adjutant was by CO's side in the afternoon and recounted the details to him. Vj regretfully offered to quit. The CO, who was in the bed because of the fever sat up and in disbelief asked Vj if he wanted to quit while confronted with an adversity. The reply can be well imagined. He directed his Adjutant that there would be no more such withdrawal sentiments/tendencies.

The next question of the unnerved youngman to his experienced CO was as to what was likely to happen. The answer needs to be quoted as accurately as possible.

> "Nothing much. I am in any case not looking forward to any more promotions. Alex can forget becoming a CO and, so far as you are concerned, we will look for job in the civil."

The CO did request a few people to help but nothing was forthcoming. The case involved an international espionage scandal, which became subsequently notorious as 'Samba Spy Case' and the escapee was one of the two initiators of the biggest espionage scandal that rocked the Indian Army.

"A sable cloud turns forth its silver lining when it is the darkest." The cordon that was established in the morning and was progressively contracting, succeeded in catching the escapee by the evening. He had dug up a fox hole and was hiding there. The man was brought back to the QG and his recapture was immediately reported. The higher HQ, however, thought differently and rightly so. The reply was "The escapee has been apprehended is fine but a serious security lapse has taken place and needs to be investigated fully." The C of I was ordered to carry on.

The days and nights that followed thereafter were the heaviest encountered by us. The whole life was down and out. The C of I blamed the Adjutant (Vj) and the lower staff for the lapse. During those days and a few days later, when Vj went to his office, he got a 'Show Cause Notice', asking him as to why disciplinary action should not be taken against him.

With the letter in his hand, he walked over to the adjacent office of his CO. He was engrossed reading something. Seeing his Adjutant enter, he looked up and asked, "So you too have got your love letter!" Well, you are not the only one—here is mine". He handed over the letter he was reading to Vj and asked him to come back with a reply. He asked his Adjutant to come back with a fair reply for him to sign and not a draft for approval. The youngman did not move and requested for a draft from the CO. The CO said, "You know my mind and I like your language, there in no need, therefore, for the draft". Vj did not move. Eventually the CO agreed and asked him to sit down and take a dictation very carefully.

> "The security lapse took place in the unit, for which I am fully responsible. My being away on leave is of no consequence. I should be held responsible and no one below me needs to be answerable. Appropriate action against me may please be taken."

Vj came out to find Major Alex sitting in his office with his love letter. Major Alex's reply was on the following lines:

> "The security lapse took place during the time I was responsible for the unit. Duration of one day is not important. Suitable action should be taken against me only and not against anyone above or below me."

While the two senior gentlemen were asked to show cause as to why Administrative Action should not be taken against them, Vj, who was directly blamed by the C of I, was asked to show cause as to why Disciplinary Action should not be initiated against him. Vj's reply was as under:

> "Being the Adjutant of the unit, QG is entirely my direct responsibility. Therefore, nobody above me or below me is may be held accountable for the security lapse that occurred. Appropriate action as deemed fit may be taken against me."

The replies were forwarded in good time and that was the last anybody heard about it. There was no more correspondence and no action was ever initiated. Unofficially, we, however, learnt that the General responsible to handle the case was about to become the next chief. He was happy with the response and, remarked that such are the bastards I want in the Indian Army-Pardon them.

They all survived and prospered and lesser minds still harp on Zero Mistake Syndrome. Ya the God does look after fools and infantry men.

❑

10

A Cleopatra Bath

The narrative has become a little too grim and that is against the tide of intended fun. No more serious interludes. Let us then quickly get down to the basic pursuit of laughing together. Talking of baths, it is generally believed that while bathing in the common bathrooms in SIKH LI, even if somebody drops a new cake of soap, no one dares to retrieve it. That notwithstanding it is a general experience that after a hard day at work, a bath is a luxury and especially if it is luxurious one.

The unit was deployed on the Ditch Cum Bundh (DCB) but some unfortunate incidents in the neighbouring unit had resulted in the ditch being declared out of bounds for bathing.

That was the time of the annual operational practice (Op Alert). It was a gruelling exercise that went on for five to six days without a break. It all went off quite well and having completed it successfully, everyone was in high spirits. Major Alex alongwith his company (approximately 150 men) was deployed on the forbidden waters and, being among the senior officers of the unit, was considered ideal to ensure the water/bath discipline.

The CO was also in a happy state of mind after successful completion of the assigned mission. He took his open jeep and alongwith his Adjutant (Vj) went to give a pat on the back of his officers. The CO was himself driving and Vj was in the co-driver's seat. From a long distance, only both of them could see a few good men on the ditch bank bathing/preparing to bath. No words were exchanged and the jeep kept reducing the distance and it was clearly visible that the law breakers were their own. As the distance shrank a little more, two of them disappeared and the third one was by then known and recognised to be none other than the Blue-eyed boy of the CO—Major Alex. He was in no position to attempt an escape. Wise man that he is, he tried evasion. He confronted the approaching Tsunami with a submarine tactics and dived inside the water evidently planning to re-emerge once the red light vehicle went past, but red lights are not given for nothing. The Old Man certainly knew a bit more. He got down from his vehicle stood right above the diving point. Major Alex, inspite of being from Kerala—one foot above sea level, did not have amphibian capability. Gradually, he started to emerge discovering his CO standing right above and looking vertically down at him like a 'Depth Charge' of Navy. Wet and decorated with a few water weeds, Major Alex completed his upwards emergence and wished his CO a Very Good Morning, who left without a word and after barely acknowledging the maritime salutation.

One could learn this art of ignoring an apparently serious lapse from the CO who always surprised everyone thus, and in many other manners.

❑

11

A Send Off Which Never Was

World has often been described as a mirror which cries if one cries in front of it and smiles back if you smile in front of it. Often the difference between a tragedy and comedy is the thought process of the subject.

The CO had a guest, a lady, who was somewhat a stuck up person. High on fashion and style but not so in social interaction, lacking the amicability of friendly rapport. Understandably, she was not very popular with the unit crowd.

Every good thing and even not so good thing comes to an end and so did her stay. She was to eventually depart to add to the woes of the National Capital, but coincidently or perhaps otherwise, the CO had to leave for an important job well before the departure time of her train. The Adjutant as always was tasked to ensure her comfortable departure. Vj apprised the CO that one of the Officers, Major Chauhan (Chau Sir, as Vj calls him) was leaving for a course in the same train and could easily and conveniently escort the lady upto Delhi. The arrangements were appreciated and the CO satisfied fully left the unit.

Major Alex was under posting and was to leave the unit during Chau's absence on course. This was enough of a reason for the two soldiers to get sentimental and they both were having their private farewell party at the lunch time, which extended uncomfortably close to the departure time of the train. By the time the twosome reached the Guest

Room to meet the lady she had already transformed into a lioness and was pacing up and down in the Guest Room as if it was a Zoo cage.

Much beyond her best, she gave them a taste of her tantrums but soldierly chivalry withstood that onslaught for she was, after all, CO's guest. They eventually left, all three of them for Major Alex thought it prudent to see off Chau, who was escorting the lady. And then, as usually happens, while enroute, the vehicle broke down, the tantrums multiplied and time to board the train further diminished.

Vehicle got repaired and the railway station was finally reached but not before the guard was already waving Green. It became difficult to identify the relevant compartment. The two officers quickly decided that the two passengers should immediately board the train and subsequently find out their reservation through the vestibule. This was not approved by the Lady but Chau entrained alongwith her ticket and rice, which she had bought to be taken home.

The train started its move. Major Alex now left one to one with the lady and asked her to board. She demanded her ticket. He told her that she will get it from Chau. She did not trust him. The interminable argument became hot, but time and tide and train wait for none and it moved away and fast. The warring twosome was now standing on the platform sans the train, accusing each other of the irresponsibility. Major Alex eventually told her that the person tasked to take her had already reached the next station and he was not the one to have been entrusted with this task. He clarified to her that he was there, only per chance and that she should mind her language and behaviour, and, as a last concession, he offered her a drive back to the Unit Guest Room.

She evidently understood the 'No Go' situation and accepted the repulsive offer. Back to square one, Major Alex spoke to Vj about the 'Great Train Miss' and the 'Miss Back'. The CO returned and learnt it all first from her and only then from his Adjutant. There was still some time left for the Indian Airlines flight to Delhi and she was ultimately seen off by Air. Then CO in his inimitable style ignored it all including the financial loss, and the matter ended, but it did not end, three to four days later, a telegram was received from Chau:

> "Lady left at Railway Station.
> Rice with MCO Delhi."
> (MCO is Movement Control Organization, which is an Army Detachment at Important Railway Stations)

The CO handed over the telegram to Vj: "Bloody chap does not even allow me to forget it all."

❑

12

Another Cleopatra

> *"Smile from reasons flow.*
> *To brute denied.*
> *And are of love – the food."*
>
> **–Milton**

The unit had got its second CO, Lt Col KS Bindra. The Colonel and his wife were both a very affectionate couple and we started to gel well and increasingly well with time.

It was once again the Annual Operational Alert and the unit was deployed to practise its Operational Role. CO's residential tent was erected a little away from the Battalion Headquarters and in the intimate protection of the depth company commanded by none other than Chau. Now back from the course as narrated in the previous chapter.

During the Exercise itself once at about 8 o'clock in the morning, the Adjutant got a call from Chau, inquiring about CO's programme, his basic interest being whether the CO was visiting his company or not. Vj confirmed to him that the CO was to proceed to the Higher Headquarters and was not likely to visit him and he, therefore, need not wait for him.

After the Adjutant had briefed the CO of all the events that had been unfolding tactically, the CO prepared to leave for the Brigade Headquarters but then he realised that he had forgotten his glasses. Vj confirmed from the CO if he could send anyone to collect his glasses from his living accommodation. The CO, however, felt that since his tent was enroute to the Brigade Headquarters, he would pick up his glasses himself and proceed from there itself, and thereby not lose any time.

Meanwhile, Chau had felt differently. He thought now that the Old Man was away and unlikely to return early, why not indulge in an elaborate Cleopatrish bath in CO tent. Ample water, good bathmat, effective drainage and best privacy, were too dangerous attractive propositions to be ignored and he decided to allow himself that luxury.

The famous bath was in progress. Chau had generated rich lather of soap on his massive, not too shapely figure, when the CO entered to collect his glasses, unmindful of what was happening in the rear echelons of his accommodation.

Chau, however, realised that the water could any moment become Waterloo and without wasting any more precious time lifted the rear most flap of the bath tent crawled through it fully lathered with soap from top to bottom, no toes and with a very generous application of local dust and grass consequent to his crawling out escaped. Once liberated the fully lathered man ran hell for leather and succeeded in his Great Escape. Mercifully, the CO did not feel the necessity or urge to visit his bathtent and oblivious of all the mishaps occurring in the inner courts, collected his glasses and went away.

Having cleaned up and dried himself, Chau rang up the Adjutant and had a real fight with him as to why was he given wrong information.

Such incidents enjoy secrecy for a limited time frame only and are shared thereafter with everyone to laugh together. The whole unit and the CO himself came to know about this misadventure subsequently and the result was only another session of laughing together.

❑

13

Another Waterfall

"Good humour is the best article of dress one can wear in society."

—William Makepeace Thakerey

We were in a location which was opened to usage for the first time. It was indeed a very comfortable and good stay and very eventful too as must have been already realised by my readers. On the whole with all its pluses and minuses it was very enjoyable.

Unit locations in Service are called Key Location Plan (KLP) like all equipment even KLP follows what is commonly and in management jargon called 'Bath Tub Curve'. There were many problems concerning the civil engineering aspects of construction and the seniors in the unit as also above it were justifiably far from amused. The biggest, nay, the tallest eyesore was a tall overhead water tank that became our own 'Water fall' exclusively because of the leakage it developed.

During that period, the General, who had earlier forgiven the unit in the espionage case, decided to visit the unit. He was a respected figure and the CO wanted nothing short of the best to be displayed before him. Preparations for the visit had commenced well before time and in real earnest. The unit was working proverbially 25 hours a day and everything was at its best for the visit.

Young Sepoy Lal Singh had had enough and decided to give it all a miss by delinking for a day without taking any leave of absence. This is an offence under the Army Act and due cognisance of it was taken. Preparations for the big day had progressed without anyone missing their 'Lal' for Lal was no kingpin.

The big day dawned and the General was briefed in great details. He was happy with the performance of the unit and everyone also was heaving a great sigh of relief. The visit was about to complete when the carcade came near the leaking giant of a structure. The Big Man did not like the inefficient structure in a new KLP. He demanded an explanation from the Chief Engineer (CE) accompanying him. The CE tried his best to explain but failed to convince him. The General most unexpectedly started to climb the steps leading spirally around the tank upwards. Since the seniormost officer was moving up the whole accompanying entourage likewise started to climb. The CO was the juniormost in that hierarchy and took his turn to climb.

We all know such Water Tanks. They are usually 60 to 80 ft tall with only one staircase and that is the only route of ingress. As the General reached above, young Lal Singh in the SIKH LI trademark red underwear, with his well-massaged and well-toned muscular body and well-oiled open hair stood up and very smartly wished the General a 'Sat Sri Akal'.

Everyone was taken aback. The withdrawal was hasty and quiet. The General had seen whatever he wanted to and also whatever he did not want to. Such visits are generally followed by a lunch to unwind. The rest of the officers who were not part of the entourage and the ladies had already reached the Officers' Mess and were waiting for the arrival of the General. Meanwhile, whatever had happened up above the world so high was known to all and had started impacting the party mood adversely.

The General sensed the prevailing apprehensions and told the CO in the hearing of everyone not to punish that boy for his initiative and ingenuity in getting away from what must have been happening in the unit is worth appreciating. He added that it was his mistake to have gone where he was least or not at all expected.

❑

14

Deserting a Colleague Under Fire

"That Commander is skillful in defence whose enemy does not know where to attack and that Commander is skillful in attack whose enemy does not know what to defend."

– Sun Tzu

Sun Tzu perhaps did not realise that all strategic and tactical thoughts degenerate into irrelevance when the enemy springs up from integral resources and seizes the initiative and surprise. The only time I have seen the hitherto much applauded team disintegrate and desert a colleague under effective fire while struggling in a mine field also needs to be recounted for, otherwise it may be a self-inflicted moral aspersion, because if I narrate the positives, I must be equally fair in reporting the negatives.

Major SP Singh (SP) and his wife, Vandana were a loveable couple, very cooperative and always willing to join in the interest of the team and the unit. Poor SP could hardly ever imagine that he would be left high and dry, actually down and out during the time of his actual need.

The route from the unit lines to the road-head could match the worst stretches of North Africa and while Rommel negotiated those in the tanks we were to go across that mine field in our 150 cc two wheelers. Some very deft handling could only see the drivers and the riders emerge unscathed.

It was a pleasant winter afternoon and all of us had decided to go together for a cup of coffee in the only Five

Star Hotel of the town. It is a typical and strange habit of this entirely different set of humans, in spite of very tight pockets, they often take recourse to such elaborate indulgence.

We were on our respective two wheelers. Those were not the days of cars. The Maruti revolution was nowhere on the horizon and a scooter was the prize possession which would be available through the Canteen Stores Department (CSD) after an unending wait of five years and for a prohibitive sum of ` 2,900/-. Coming back on course we were all moving across the unit gate in our best attire one after another. Those were also the days when women still wore saris and men wore suits with ties/scarves. As Vj cut across the most dicey turn, we saw SP lose control of his Lambretta and it fell albeit in a slow motion. Hapless Vandana, in her best sari and with her best purse, was on the pillion and saris did not permit women to ride crossed leg. She tumbled equally in slow motion on the other side on her back. Realising that others would be following, she very rapidly recovered and stood up but SP was still struggling to retrieve the scooter. That was the precise time when that fat purse transformed into a lethal weapon and started falling on his head, shoulders, face and wherever possible. He did not know how to tackle it and had surprisingly lost the art of escape and evasion. Running extremely deficient of arms and hands for at that moment he required many more—one to retrieve the scooter, one to dust his suite, one to retrieve his glasses and many more to shield from the ceaseless straffing.

We drew nearer and Vj drove past just by waving at the warring couple and shouting 'All the Best'. Could there be anything meaner?

❑

15

The New Launge (Long) Suit

"Robbed that smiles, steals something from the thief."
—Shakespeare

Pay Commission arrears had finally arrived and the windfall had suddenly accorded us a much needed financial elbow space. I prevailed upon Vj (as I always do) and we bought a suit-length for him and got it stitched from the best tailor in the town, who took about three months and most of the balance of pay commission arrears but did make him look nice for a change.

The new suit had co-incidently got timed with a party in the Officers' Mess for which the dress code was Long Suit (as the men called it). Vj was understandably happy for he would be able to show case his best turn out. He instructed his helper to get the suit ironed and bring it back on a hanger to retain its crease.

In the evening, when we were dressing up for the party, Vj wore his new suit but found his pant much too long and had no idea how to manage it. It was another good opportunity for me to let him have it for having avoided the trial at the tailor's shop. He pleaded not guilty for he had indeed gone for the trial but unimpressed I told him that mere going was not enough and trial had to be an elaborate affair. He had to concede and, eventually, the good old 'NARA' came to his rescue and we were ready to leave. But almost simultaneously there was a more dire fire fight across the road where Captain Jaipal Malik lived. His suit as per what we could decipher from his shouting had got washed by his helper and had shrunk to barely below his knees. The helper was, however insisting that he had not got it washed but had only got it ironed, but then the shrinkage was too pronounced to be missed. Jaipal eventually outshouted the man into silence and arrived at the party looking like Raj Kapoor of 50s inspite of having worn the pant like modern day low waisted jeans. The party commence but both men were visibly uncomfortable. Somehow the predicament unfolded in my mind and I called Vj but he would not listen and was as usual too engrossed in the music. I eventually went to Jaipal and asked him to drag Vj to the nearby Guest Room and interchange their suits.

Actually, both the suit-lengths two gentlemen were done by a lady from Dhariwal which was closer to her village and had the same colour and same fabric and were even stitched by the same tailor. The suits had got interchanged by the Dhobi where those were taken for ironing. There was no washing/shrinking and there was no need for the 'NARA' Vj wore.

❑

16

The Good Turnout

"Man is the only creature endowed with the power to laugh."
—Greville

Talking of suits and turnout, there is another interesting episode *albeit* in different circumstances that deserves a mention.

There was a long patrol. Long Range Patrol (LRP), as they call it, and quite a few officers and men including Vj went on it. The objective was terrain familiarization and it was to take approximately three weeks.

After the LRP was out for about a week plus they lost contact with the unit and considering the areas where they were operating, it became a rather curious situation. None however voiced it but everyone was consoling and comforting everyone, but then as he always maintains that 'God looks after fools and infantrymen', the contact got re-established a few days later. We learnt that they were well and had got encircled in some very inclement weather and were no longer in a position to move ahead or withdraw. After another couple of anxious days, the weather presented a window of opportunity and they were heli-lifted back to civilization. Those were the days when Dimple Kapadia as Bobby was ruling the glam world. Once back into civilization, the youngsters in the LRP prevailed upon the seniors to go straight to see Bobby and, in the true team spirit, it was agreed.

One of the officers was however deputed to request all of the ladies to join them at the theatre. Everybody played up and got ready for the experience had taught us that such rare opportunities ought to be grabed. None however realised that the menfolk must be in the dirtiest of conditions—unwashed, unshaven and stinking to say the least.

We reached the theatre and by that time, the movie had moved closer to the interval, but who was interested in the movie? The focus was on reunion and meeting the survivors, for whom nothing unusual had happened.

We approached the gatekeeper and inquired if some officers had gone in and had left any message for us. He was not amused and, in fact, must have been a very arrogant and rude man. He shot back, "I do not know if they are officers but some very dirty looking faujis had got in to watch the movie and had not even bought the tickets, which were to be bought by us". Well, that was Turnout to say the least.

Needless to say, we bought the tickets and enjoyed whatever was left of the movie.

❑

17

The Bollywood Linkages

"Smile costs nothing but creates much' is a famous proverb but, in this case, it cost me a lot and created only fake relationships.

Yogita Bali was the starlet of late 60s and early 70s, who, to my relief, fizzled out without much of a mark, but in the unit, she was recognised to be Vj's sister and, thus, my sister-in-law. Simi Grewal was similarly linked to Major Grewal and we were morally and socially obliged to foot the bills of all their movies, which irrespective of their cinematic quality, were seen by all the officers and their wives. There was hardly any choice with us. Luckily, for both of us Grewals and Balis, both Simi Grewal and Yogita Bali were not great success. Had it been Hema Bali and Rekha Grewal, we would have had some real tough financial times and would have had to withdraw still more frequently from the 'Defence Services Officers' Provident Fund (DSOP) or Unit Baniya. Financial predicaments notwithstanding what hurt more was the choice of roles the two ladies choose to perform, which, to say the least, were not very sisterly and, for this very reason, we were subjected to some intense psychological torment.

While our knowledge of movies and actors was till then quite up-to-date and complete, the Grewals were actually more into religion and Gurdwara and Simi Grewal was, thus, more embarrassing than our sister, for being bolder of the two and boldest of that era.

During those days, TV was only restricted to 'Krishi Darshan' and 'Chitrahar' and, therefore, for the entertainment of the troops, the Higher Headquarters used to send Cinema Section (Mobile Cinema) to the unit. The Cinema Section generally used to bring two movies, out of which the unit could select one depending upon its choice. It was then a totally captive affair, the movie, or a particular scene or a song could be rescreened again and again.

On one such day, the Cinema Section arrived and, as is the norm, reported to the Adjutant. It was already lunch time and the CO had started walking towards his residence. Vj told Major Grewal that the Cinema Section had arrived and that he would apprise the CO about it. Major Grewal, the 2IC in a mock anger, objected, "Why, welfare is my subject, I will tell the CO." The junior man—Adjutant had to say, "Yes Sir".

By that time, the CO had gained some more distance towards his residence. Both the 2IC and the Adjutant caught up with him and he stopped. The 2IC spoke, "Sir, the Cinema Section has come and I think we can screen a movie in the evening at about 1900 hours, if it is okay with you." The CO said okay and then uncharacteristically inquired, "Which movie?" "Sir, there are two movies; whichever' you desire, we will have it screened." "Which are the movies, Garry?" the CO inquired. The 2IC replied—"Sir, one is Reshma and the other is Shera." The CO knew better—"Garry 'Reshma aur Shera'" is one movie only. There only the 2IC turned to address the Adjutant, "Bloody Man, you never told me so."

❑

18

The Cricket Glory

Two men from SIKH LI were watching a well attended Cricket Match. After sitting for some time, their patience wore off and one of them remarked to his companion, "What useless teams are playing—there is no goal scored even in two hours." A cricket enthusiast sitting next to them gave them a dirty look and the wiser of the two understood that there was something amiss. He quickly corrected his junior with a rebuke. "Stupid, they are not playing Basketball to be scoring goals." This attracted another dirty glance and the chap also asked them if they had no clue about the games, why they were wasting their time there. Natha quickly shot back, "Why, we know all the games. There are but just three games." The surprised stranger asked them as to what those three games were. Pat came the answer, "Hockey, Football and Tournament." To this, the senior of the two added that there were only three teams in the whole world playing those three games. The bemused stranger asked, "Which were those three teams?" "India, Pakistan and Foreign" was the confident answer.

Above notwithstanding the big boss from the Higher Headquarter, who had recently taken over the Brigade, desired an Inter-unit Cricket Tournament. Vj was the only man in the unit who had played cricket in his younger days and, in fact, it was entirely due to his cricket expertise that most academics were like 'tournament' to him. He was, therefore, tasked to form, train and lead the Cricket team of the unit. Selection of 11 men from 1,000 extremely fit men might appear to be an easy task but notwithstanding their expertise in the field, was a tall order.

Man, who was a goal keeper in hockey or football, was considered appropriate to be the wicket keeper. Men, who had gone on NCC for a tenure and had seen boys play cricket, were automatically selected and eventually a team got formed.

The next problem was to have 11 sets of white dresses for the match. Men are not indeed fond of wearing 'whites' and surely there was no Naval Ship in the neighbourhood. This road block was also negotiated successfully with the great help coming from the unit cooks and bandsmen.

Players, who were from the hockey fraternity, were too confident, for if they could stop, hit and manipulate a ball with the narrow blade of a hockey stick, to miss it with the broad blade of a cricket bat, was unthinkable. Kindly imagine their bewilderment when the first ball they faced landed on the wickets or in the hands of the goal/wicket keeper.

The match commenced and, apart from the quality of the game, every other thing was in super class. The ground, the pitch, the equipment and the spectators. Some theoretical and practical knowledge had been imparted to the potential cricketers, which all proved to be of little value once the toss was over. Luckily, Vj's team had to field first and, thus, came to acquire the experience of seeing the other side bat, but once the other team finished their innings, many thought that the match was over and had started changing and packing to leave. They were, of course, held back.

The batting began and a few of the batsmen, who were less clueless, took the team's score perilously close to winning, for after all the opponents too were not Kapils, Sunils or Sachins. Ultimately, there were two great batsmen at the crease, who had excelled in by all the pre-match coaching and training. The ball was bowled and was thrashed beyond the 'long on'. The twosome stood rooted to their respective crease, watching the ball roll. Some others might have thought it to be arrogance of a Sehwag but Vj knew better and he shouted from the makeshift Pavillion, 'Bhago Oye' (Run You Chaps) and they instantaneously obeyed. While the batsman, who had hit the shot, ran towards the non-striker's end the non-striker, who had earlier been appreciated for his fielding, ran the hardest towards the ball and almost succeeded in preventing it from crossing the boundary, inspite of all that he wore (pads, gloves and guards) and carried (bat).

❑

19

The Common Life

"None is so affluent who can live without the goodwill or so poor who cannot pass it on."

– Anonymous

It was truly amazing to see these interesting men gel so well. No rat race, no under-the-belt shots but only a commitment to belong whole-heartedly to each other. A complete symbiosis.

We had a scooter but it belonged to all those officers, who did not have one and was called by them as our scooter. Vj and me enjoyed no priority rights on it. We could get it in our turn or by the draw of lots.

There were a few of them who had the proverbial fish-like capacity to drink and sometimes go over their top. Vj was and is a square peg—'a teetotaller and had deviced a successful methodology to control the higher state of mind of his drinking friends. He would get drunk exclusively on 'Coca Cola' and would turn forth such award-winning realistic performance, that convinced not only the strangers but also the ones who knew him well and had drunk themselves high. They all had to then control Vj, whose act of drunkardness was no less than that of Amitabh's later day masterpiece in 'Amar, Akbar, Anthony'. At times, in the beginning, I too was misled into believing that he had taken what he said he never does. I later came to know that during one of his such moods, in his bachelor days, he had insisted on getting married there and then, and with the daughter of the local Halwai, the vested interest being only the sweets he made. He was, in fact, taken to the residence of that Halwai as suiter of his daughter unmindful of her other attributes. The poor but otherwise quite rich Halwai regretted truly or falsely that he had no daughter, if only he had one, I could have been saved from what I got.

I also recollect his such later act. A lady, whose husband had recently joined the unit, told him very genuinely that "Capt Bali, I will talk to you in the morning." Next evening, we called on them and she was embarrassed no end to know that the drunkard she was avoiding the previous night was only play acting.

❑

20

Near Bout with Dara Singh

Once you know yourself and know your opponent, there is a chance of succeeding but not at all if you are Vj and opponent is the greatest wrestler of all times – Dara Singh.

Vj was detailed to attend a course at Pune and we moved together and, at the same time, the unit moved to its next field area, but we shall talk about Pune first.

It was an illogically busy course and we were living in the Officers Mess. There was another gentleman. He too was living with his family and had hired a private accommodation at a distance little away from the institute. He was finding it hard to cope with the curriculum and decided to move to a house much closer to the school. Our finances as always were also under strain and we decided to move to the accommodation vacated by him, particularly since Vj was not overly burdened by the course.

Once the sequential shift was affected and I was at our new abode all by myself, the officer who had vacated the accommodation came knocking at the door. I opened the bolt and asked the gentleman in, thinking that perhaps he had forgotten something, but the poor chap got embarrassed for so bogged down was he with the work pressure that he had forgotten the fact of having shifted from there.

Another evening, I wanted to see a picture but Vj was more interested in the Wrestling Bout of Dara Singh that was scheduled to be held at Pune. One of those rare things, I relented and both of us went to see the great wrestler in action live. The arena was full and lesser fights were progressing and to say the least I was not finding them very arrestive but somewhere within perhaps there was a desire to see the iconic wrestler live and that kept me from leaving.

Eventually, the great man arrived to a very rousing fanfare. He entered the ring and was disrobing to come into his real tough and imposing being when suddenly there was an announcement on the Public Address (PA) system: "Major Bali, wherever you are, please reach the ring side immediately. I was astonished beyond limits, had this irrational misadventurist sitting by my side challenged Dara Singh, but was relieved to discover surprise on his face too but by then I had already rebuked him with my unthinkable apprehensions. We decided to ignore the call but then it was being repeated again and again. He decided to put an end to it all and stood up to brave it. He headed towards Dara Singh with me in the tow.

Soon we were there at the striking distance from the strongest man on the globe whose half a slap could put both of us to eternal peace. To our inexplicable surprises and relief, we found Flt Lt Daljit Taneja, Vj's childhood friend, waiting for us there. The call was from him. He had come to Pune on a flying trip and had gone to our house only to find it locked and knew without doubt and immediately as to where to find him/us.

I was once again surprised to find how much and how well these men knew each other. Only if they had channelised their energies better!

❑

21

Dual Danger

"A smile is rest to the weary, daylight to the discouraged, sunshine to sad and nature's best antidote for trouble."

– Anonymous

But it vanishes when confronted with the type of threats that manifest quite frequently in the lifestyle chosen by some of us.

Having traversed the complete breadth of the country, the unit had reached its new location where we joined them after successfully surviving both, that meaningless course and that gentle giant—the star of every Indian Eye—Dara Singh.

Interestingly, our new location was a place with zero pollution. No dust, no noise, and not even lights. After last light, the number of stars was well matched by the number of Glow Worms on the earth and it was well neigh impossible to establish which way the numerical superiority lay. Trumpeting of elephants, hissing of snakes and other wild sounds had become quite a normal part of natural accoustics and we were fast getting well acclimatized to it all.

In such situation, some kind of unwelcoming experiences are always a very likely proposition. That was our such day. We were returning from the house of a distant relative after a late lunch. Late afternoons in those areas are almost evenings. It was about 4 pm and had begun to get dark and we two as usual were on our old faithful Bajaj

150-Scooter in the dust tracks of the Tea Estate when some wild big cat jumped over us, at least that is what we felt and, without any trace, vanished into the bushes. We knew cheetahs to be extinct, we also knew the lions are only in Gir Forest, we also knew that we were not in a Tiger Reserve, but a leopard or a panther is bad enough to sort out anybody's happiness in those areas and we certainly knew them to be local residents. It was terribly unnerving for both of us but we braved it all well (as if there was a choice). Our host's house was not very far from there but I confess that the Infantry Soldier had already impacted even me and never did we consider the possibility of turning back to him much less to spend the night with him.

We pressed on about another kilometer down the track and discovered a huge black speed breaker lying against the whole breadth of the country road, which must have been minimum six to eight feet. My zoology, of which I was very proud and I still am, failed to identify in that fading light whether we were confronting a python or a king cobra, but that was of little relevance. Whatever it was, it was there and we did not know how to negotiate across it and bypassing was prevented by the thick tea bushes. Eventually, Vj decided to drive over it. I was not impressed with that bravado and suggested that we wait a little bit and it may move across. Vj was also constantly blowing the scooter horn and I had to put him wise by telling him that the 'Blacky' had no ears. He, however, told me that the music he was constantly generating was not for the chap who was lying on the road but for the one who could have been in the bushes around us and could try a more accurate jump on us. The beauty on the road was in no hurry and the thought of the other close by in the bushes clinched the issue and we got ready to drive over it. Chilled down to the spine and even deeper, we successfully negotiated the speed breaker. We did not bother to look back as to what injury or discomfort we had inflicted on it. No 'Ichchhadhari Nagin', has since been chasing us, so we infer that alongwith us they too survived.

Back in our lodgings we changed and went to sleep as early as we could. Our beds were spread in the rear courtyard formed by erecting the canvass side walls of a tent. After I was adequately rested, I noticed that my feet were at a higher elevation than my head and the man alongside was also in a similar posture. I nudged at him to voice my observation but he was least impressed and asked me to forget the plains of the peace areas and get used to the undulating life of the underdeveloped field areas. He once again went to sleep after delivering his moral lecture but I was quite uncomfortable for the rest of the night, which was quite natural after the day I had.

Like last light, even the first light is also quite early in those areas and when we could see the surroundings we discovered that we were sleeping on the beds spread upside down. The head and the foot rests were on the ground and the four legs were threatening to penetrate the clouds and bring down fresh rains which, in any case were never in shortage. Luckily, because of the privacy improvised by the side walls of the tents, nobody other than some wild monkeys saw us sleeping or waking up in such lop-sided posture. The genesis of the bed spread is not of importance.

❑

22

A Transistor : Once Upon a Time

A time comes in the life of a person when he or she begins to laugh at his/her own difficulties, through long acquaintance with them, and it comes rather fast in Army life for every dawn ushers in fresh events which, if thought about positively, can be laughed at but, if allowed to impact feelings, can be quite the opposite, though the equation is not always that simplistic.

Those were the days when transistor had replaced the radios and were the status symbol. The transistor revolution was something like the mobile telephones of today. Television was still restricted to a few metros and 'Krishi Darshan' drew packed crowds. The place where we were was certainly too 'door' for 'Doordarshan' and our only linkage to the outside world was the good old transistor which served us faithfully 24 × 7.

One day after rendering a yeoman's service, uninterrupted for more than a decade, our world link went quiet and for us it became a very disquietening period. A quick change of battery a few slaps here and there failed to resuscitate the little thing, but then every infantry battalion has its own 'Electronic Engineer', who can repair anything and everything that responds to electricity. He was called to do the needful and he arrived with due urgency to attend to Adjutant's transistor. Expressing total confidence, he committed to do the job within the next 24 hours.

The next day we were all sitting in the common varandah sipping our evening tea when Naik Sohan Singh, our electronics expert arrived. Our transistor very proudly slung to his shoulders and good old Mohammad Rafi singing one of his many hit songs.

He handed over the transistor to me with a little wire of about four inches sticking out of it. He explained it as an antenna he had installed for improved performance because of the distance involved from the broadcasting station. We both appreciated his ingenuity, expertise and innovation and thanked him for the job well done and that too in such a record time. Vj was visibly proud on the performance of his blue-eyed boy, who was happy to have received the commendation.

Before delinking the great expert, however, put his hand in the pocket of his short which extended well below his knees and well above his ankles, and took out a fistful of small nuts and screws and handed them over to Vj's Helper with very deliberate instructions to keep those safe, for those were the spare parts retrieved from the poor transistor, who continued to play flawlessly.

❑

23

The Great Awareness

Knowledge, wise men, say is never complete and there is no end to not knowing. Ignorance is many a times nothing short of bliss and then there is God who looks after fools and infantry men and by implication all those who are foolish enough to tie the knot with infantrymen.

Stay in that country of elephants and apes was mercifully not too long. Vj got another course and we were at Hyderabad where Vj's younger sister Varsha got married to Flt Lt Sudhir Chaitanya and Vj's friend, Daljit of 'Dara Singh' fame were already posted. Major Basith, whose famous 'Dog Encounter' I have already narrated, had by then shifted to IPS and was also there. All of us were together painting the town red and our respective bank balances were also perpetually in red. None of us realised that such princely compatibility required less mismatching financial back up. Many a times, in fact, rather frequently, it became hard to bridge the non-availability breach. It was a sorry state towards the end of every month with a joint wait for the next month's pay.

During this time, Vj got his first staff posting and they all proclaimed it to be good for him. People were complimenting and felicitating us but I did not understand as to what earth shaking achievement it was, because I had failed to locate the place of his new posting on any map or globe. Sudhir understood my problem and showed me the place on the Air Force service map. I was still not impressed.

We were now to delink from the unit and form our first home away from it and run it ourselves without any support from the friends and assistance from the seniors, who, to say the least, were like another family. Vj used to call his unit as his first family because he used to spend 10 months in a year in the unit as against 2 months he had at home, if at all.

We prepared to reach our new station. While Vj went to his unit to do his official departure formalities, I went to Delhi to get all the household items ready and packed. A few days later, he came back to Delhi and together we embarked on our momentous journey.

Papa was now in a very influential position and the whole "Brake Van' of the train was made available to us to load our stuff. We had no packing material and lesser packing experience. Our refrigerator was lying in the Brake Van as if it was under use of the Railway staff.

Next morning, we reached our detraining station and were to proceed approximately 100 km from there on road. Transport alongwith a few men to unload and reload our stuff were there to receive us on the platform. They emptied the compartment and the luggage van in no time and I counted it all to find everything in order. For going to the road head, the luggage had to be taken across two to three platforms, the other choice was to lug it across the overhead bridge. First option was preferred for obvious reasons. As the men were moving the luggage across the Railway lines, both of us decided to take the longer route over the bridge and perhaps also had a pause for a cup of tea.

By the time we reached the road head, all our luggage was already across and was in the process of being loaded on the lorry. Just as a confirmatory and rapport building words, Vj asked the group commander if everything had been got from the detraining platform. "O yes Sir, everything has been moved this side and loaded but for one 'Bottle Thermos'." We were both surprised for we did not possess any flask and much less the one so big that required a deliberate coverage. Meanwhile the mystery 'Bottle Thermos' arrived – it was our Cooking Gas Cylinder. That also speaks a lot about our own awareness level. No Transfer Voucher, we carried the cylinder itself and that too in the luggage van of the train and even with some gas still in it to commence cooking immediately on arrival.

Those were the days when all Vacuum Flasks were called Thermos, all toothpastes were known as Colgate and all bathing soaps as Lifeboy – no there was no 'U' in the Buoy, and, therefore, equating Gas Cylinder to a Bottle Thermos was not exactly out of place.

❑

24

The Experienced Witch

A woman went and bought a water melon. As she cut it to have it, a Gini appeared with folded hands, and asked her directions to perform any task that she wished. The woman was delighted and asked the Gini if it was like the Gini of Alladin. Affirmative was the reply. She again asked if her Gini could also do what his senior did for Alladin. It was again affirmative. The woman felt delighted and asked the Gini to make available a regal mansion for her to stay. The Gini shot back and pleaded for pertinence from his mistress saying that he himself was living in a water melon, how the hell his mistress expected her to make a mansion for her. The point to note is that even Ginis and, at times, even Ghosts and Witches are helpless.

History (His-story) proverbially repeats itself, but in this episode, 'Her story' or 'My story' repeated itself but luckily only partly. We had settled down in our new environments. Our Gas Cylinder was burning and we had even acquired a Vacuum Flask (Thermos). Life was on course.

Then, one day, Vj had to proceed on some temporary duty (TD) for about 10 days, at the place where we had detrained for that was their Higher Headquarters. A few days passed but all by myself it had become quite boring. I, therefore, decided to visit him on the weekend and joined him there. It was a distance of approximately 100 km and was connected by a Meter Gauge (MG) train which took round about three hours.

All good things come to an end and so did the weakend. I was to return in the same train. I entrained at about 7 pm and was due to reach at 10 pm where I was to be received and taken to my house. The Railway Station, where I was to get down, used to be activated only twice in 24 hours and functioned on good old lanterns and flags. As is natural, the weekend and specially the day of departure was rather hectic and perhaps, for the only time in my life, I slept while travelling alone and I overslept and by the time I woke up, the train had left my lantern lit Railway Station behind.

There were not very many people in the compartment but a few good men came to my rescue and we started wrestling with the emergency chain. Mercifully, it worked but by the time we succeeded in brining the train to a halt, we had moved 2 to 3 km and that was bad and far enough in those areas and in those times, to be in the thick of nowhere and in darkness. In those areas, it is raining most of the times. Luckily, at that time, it was not very torrential and, in fact, was only a drizzle. The TINA (There is no alternative) factor manifested and I got down and the train moved on.

Those were the days women had not yet taken to wearing shoes and I was in a much Indian attire—a sari and high heels. And now a repeat of Pachmarhi was staring me in the face. That day or that night I realised the difference between 'One' and 'Two'. I have never missed my Worse Half (Vj) more. Thanking God for the small mercies, there were no apes and a major navigational aid was available in the shape of the Railway Line and since I could see the dim lights of the cantonment on the horizon, the distance too did not appear to be very daunting. Notwithstanding that wild and anti-social threat was always there and had already unnerved me a lot. As Field Martial Sam Manekshaw used to say, 'Fear is a natural reaction and those who claim to be not having it are either wild or Gurkhas', but I am neither. I also learnt that day that bravery too is circumstantial.

Curtesy Pachmarhi, I was certainly an experienced witch and I decided to do exactly the same in self-defence. I opened my hair and let my 'Pallu' loose and fly as much as the met conditions permitted and started my solitary walk on the Railway Line. Walking on the Railway track with a wet sari, high heel, and a bag on the shoulders at night, in a drizzle, irrespective of the distance, was not a very comfortable exercise, but then as another Field Martial (Slim) said, "things could always be worse". I did not twist an ankle, was not hungry and was not tired. That night the actual ghosts and witches had taken an off and the wild elements, both men and animals, were not interested in getting wet. The distance also proved to be shorter than anticipated, but all the same, it was not easy enacting a 'Sadhana' (the most famous actor to have enacted Ghost) and no matter how hard I tried, I could not sing. Nevertheless, I reached in the safe zone once again wet, once again tired, once again scared but this time mercifully not sick.

❑

25

A Journey Well Escorted

A boy had prepared an essay on a Football Match but it was the Railway Journey that was asked in the examination. He began by writing that as his Railway Journey commenced, the Railway engine got derailed and the train had to stop there for a long time. There was a Football match being played in the adjoining ground and, thus, the Football match was narrated in full. In my case, however, I have no necessity to prepare a Railway Journey, for the one I had, can never be erased or even diluted, from the memory.

Coming back to the main course, a few months after my nocturnal witchcraft, our little daughter arrived. Coincidently, both of us had thought of the same name separately for her. It did not take even a minute for little Pragati to get her name. In the MH, where she was born, was a panther cub under treatment. While that was a panther, our child was called a lion and it was only helped by the appointment code of the job that Vj held.

My in-laws (Mama and Bauji—another retired soldier) were there with us and the four of us together had a great time with our bundle of joy and then, as usual, I expressed a desire to visit my parents in Delhi. Bauji most readily decided to accompany me while Mama decided to stay back with her son. Accordingly, two berths were booked in AC-II. Then came a signal (Army equivalent of a telegram), Captain Jaipal Malik along with his wife and daughter was to come to us enroute to Delhi and was subsequently to move in the same train in which Bauji and me were to go. These were thought to be excellent arrangements for now both Bauji and me were to have a young escort and even good friendly company.

The friendly Malik team arrived, stayed for a few days and proceeded to see a nearby hill station. They were programmed to link with us at the Railway Station from where we all were to proceed together. On the appointed date as planned, Vj organized a truck One Ton (the most unreliable vehicle I have ever known but had not known till then), and we all started for the rail head in rather good time. I do not recollect the number of times the wretched vehicle broke down but Vj knew better and visualizing it all, he had taken a Vehicle Mechanic along who managed the battle worthy vehicle to reach the Railway Station in time, but just in time. Jaipal however, did one better and had not arrived even till then.

We barely beat the 'Guard Green' and boarded the train. Jaipal, his wife and his daughter (as old as ours) were not yet on the scene, but suddenly dawned from nowhere alongwith a porter in tow. He hurriedly had a word with Vj who had already done his leave taking with us and detrained. Most hurriedly their luggage was thrown in, Raj, carrying her infant daughter, Shalu, jumped in, followed by the young servant they were taking along and then came the delayed soldier. By this time, all the preliminaries for the move of the train were over and the wheels began to roll. Vj who as usual does not keep any money very sheepishly asked me to pay the porter that I had never hired, from the window. I refused to pay the porter with whom I had nothing to do but Vj was insisting and the train was moving and Vj was walking along. I found this demand absolutely outrageous, particularly when my own coffers were thin or almost empty. Now running to keep up with the moving window, he made me realise that Jaipal had only Re. 0.5/- or 50 paise left with him. All this discussion on a rapidly diminishing platform. Vj was running, the porter was running, Jaipal was helplessly watching. Bauji was already snoring, and I eventually relented and parted with, *albeit* most reluctantly with some most precious bills. The train had by then left Vj and porter for behind haggling over the money and there was no formal bye bye.

It was decided among the four of us that the two soldiers would move over to the First Class and the two of us, Raj and me, alongwith our infant girls, will travel in the AC compartment.

Having realised our great fiscal situation, it was decided among four of us that we would only have two 'Thalis of Meals', but the servant boy, who was accorded the supreme luxury of one full Thali, protested and wanted two. That tested Jaipal's pursuasive skills. As the famine conditions were being negotiated, the TTI found out that the servant's ticket was invalid and he asked Jaipal to pay his penalty fare. I had a total black out and my escort too was in no better health. This brought Bauji to the fore and his pursuasive talent to its best. Some pseudo links in the Railway Board came finally to our rescue and, at last, the ghastly TTI was off our collective backs.

The night descended but not the peace, for we were to now battle a fresh set of problems. The men folk had moved to the first class compartment alongwith most of the luggage, had bolted the compartment and before long were fast asleep.

This side of the Cease Fire Line (CFL) or the vestibule were four of us, Raj and me and our two infant daughters in the AC compartment's discomfort, for it became far too cold. My lopsided hygienic sense prevented us from using the Railway Bedding and we were as if on the top of the Everest. Whatever clothes and towels we had were utilised to keep the small girls cosy but the two of us were regretting having made the AC choice. Throughout the night, we kept knocking at the door of the two soldiers but they kept sleeping totally oblivious of our predicament. Those were also the days of the Bandit Queen Phoolan Devi and that was her Operational Area too which added another dimension to our nocturnal misadventure across the vestibule, and to the men folks resolve not to open the door.

Night was at last over and we survived. Never has the morning been so pleasant to me. As the uphill journey was meandering to its long awaited end. Jaipal told me that he had requested Raj's brother to receive them at the Railway Station but somehow if he failed to surface, he will request for another Rs. 50/-.

That morning on the platform, God almighty came in the form of my Pop and Raj's brother and we were all received and, thus, my well escorted journey passed into the folds of history and we all thanked God for it.

❑

26

Gandhian Approach to Third Gender

These men, about whom I have been talking, can always be credited with equality of gender and often joked about a notional matrimonial advertisement: "A smart Army Officer desirous of a life partner. No bars including that of gender". In the incident that I am presenting below, proves the equality they accord to genders—all three of them.

In due course, the mother and son team left behind also joined us in Delhi and the celebrations of little Pragati's arrival resumed within the constraints of our perpetual recession. The word had gone around and one day when I, alongwith Mama and my little daughter, were away to the temple and Bauji was away to some friend of his, the local eunuchs decided to call on us and celebrate Pragati's birth.

When the eunuch assault finally came. Vj was the only one at home, holding the fort. The relative combat strength was 1:5 in favour of the assault echelons but as is often said, numerical superiority is only one of the many factors and is certainly not decisive. Morale and intelligence can often prove to be clinching. Mahabharat was won inspite of the relative combat ratio of 7:11, whereas Indian Army works on a ratio of 1:3.

Vj answered the knock at the door with folded hands and a Namaskar that his visitors perhaps would never had received. He very seriously and with all the respect and humility invited them in and seated them in our elaborately laid out drawing room. Five of them seated on various sofas and chairs alongwith their drums, harmoniums and ghungharoos. They were already getting over awed and impressed with his civility. He then very politely informed them about the non-availability of all the other members of the family.

Not to be outdone completely, they announced their intention to wait. It was now becoming uncomfortable for him too. He said to them that they were welcome to wait but he was not sure about our likely time of return. He then offered them a cup of coffee for as he admitted and truthfully he did not know how to make a cup of tea (as if he could make coffee). The guests displayed their unfondness for the coffee and offered to brew the tea if the host did not mind their ingress into the kitchen. The access to the kitchen was graciously permitted and the eunuchs made their own tea and even for their host and had it in the best of my tea set. Perhaps they were enjoying it all. One of them also opened a packet of sweets that they had carried from their visit to the previous house and everyone including Vj enjoyed that cup of tea and Burfi, the demarcating lines between the guests and host had vanished.

They perhaps had another appointment to honour and left after a very cordial leave taking with a commitment to come back. As they were walking down the lane some distance away from our house Mama, Me and little Pragati met them. They praised Vj no ends to his mother and she also felt very proud for I know that such moments of pride from her this son must have been extremely rare.

❑

27

The House Recce

Sometimes, something may happen in a flash but its unintended impact lasts life long. Sad or happy is only a matter of opinion and my esteemed readers may draw their own conclusion about the episode I mention below, which during the prudish middle decades of the last century, would have been classified as for 'Adults Only'.

It was a Delhi Development Authority (DDA) house that we were living in and was a duplex. One of those days again when we ladies were out and the two soldiers, one retired (My father-in-law) and one serving Vj, were at home when the misfortune descended.

While the senior of the two was holding the ground floor. Vj was occupying the first floor. Bauji by then had gained quite a reputation for his sustained repose, punctuated only by his poetry composition in Urdu, which he always did with a 'Holder and an Inkpot'. The computer generation will not understand as to what those instruments were but Bauji was convinced that good 'hand writing' could not be achieved without an appropriate 'Nib'. Which script warranted which 'Nib' is unfortunately a knowledge that went away with him only.

The aforementioned scene was very peacefully passing when a woman in mid forties and on the fatish side alongwith her husband knocked at the door. Bauji asked them to move in without himself moving a bit. The couple expressed a desire to have a look-see around our house for they too were contemplating to purchase one such dwelling. The Old Soldier most willingly acceded to their request but without being disturbed from his serious literary pursuits. Their self-conducted tour was over before long for DDA does not construct 'Rashtrapati Bhavans'. Bauji, thus, very kindly offered them to have a cup of tea which they politely declined and said that they were carrying their flask. Bauji very truthfully admitted that even if they had agreed to have a cup of tea, it had to be made by the visiting lady only which he too could take. This was perhaps more than a hint for them and they decided to share the tea which they were carrying with them, *albeit* in our containers, but Bauji being the father that he was, also thought about his son (Vj) who was uptairs and was missing the grand treat. He told them about Vj's presence up above. They also wanted to see the first floor and, thus, two plus two became four.

A cup of tea was carried by the lady to the first floor for the young man alongwith her husband. Bauji did not consider it essential to do anything other than according his ready approval.

The scene on the first floor, however, was quite different. In the full knowledge of the empty house, Vj had given an elaborate massage to his young muscles and was spread on the floor like a huge crocodile and in his birth suit. The lady was leading the climb and the man was half a step too far.

The unexpected intrusion and confrontation happened and all the three participants were totally accidented. The cup of tea so considerably carried upstairs had half fallen on the floor. Vj as expected was the first to recover and regain his composure. He looked around and said, "Excuse Me" and the nearest thing he found he quietly wore, it was his elder brother's shirt and those days men wore their shirts very short and to add to that (rather subtract from it) his elder brother is almost half a foot shorter than him. The shirt could barely cover his upper portion and he then folded his hands to say in the humblest possible "Namaste".

A quick withdrawal and disengagement was affected and while the strangers retreated, the young soldier got dressed, and taking a little breather, dismounted to the presence of his father. The strangers by then had gone. Vj showed his annoyance to Bauji and explained the first floor mishap to his father, but the senior man was unmoved and advised his son to stay cool it for never again in life were they to appear in front of him, but, as he uttered these words, the battered guest, this time only the man came back asking permission to collect the cover of their flask. For sure, no one has since met them and it is now more than three decades.

❑

28

A Princely Addiction

"Laugh if you are wise." — **Martial**

One among many of the strange habits of Vj is his moving around without carrying any money in his pocket. When he was a bachelor and in his unit his 'Helper' carried his wallet and did his expenditure, and whenever that money finished, the 'Helper' had the license to take the required sum from Unit Baniya, which Vj would clear every month through a cheque without any questions and with total trust on the integrity of the men involved. While on leave, his mother or his sister would manage his money. All these responsibilities most unwillingly had to be inherited by me once I made the irrecoveable mistake of joining him for life.

That day he was to go to Connaught Place (CP) for some official work. He was to go on his scooter and it was decided between us that I will go with him till my parents house and he will come back after doing the job, he had to and, thereafter, we will come back together.

He stopped his scooter at the gate of our house and without waiting even for a second, pressed on and went away. The only thing that he had was his scooter, the oil it contained and his clothes, and those were not the days of mobile phones that I could ring him up and call him back or at least apprise him of his pauperhood. The situation was irretrieveable and he was not even aware of it.

He reached CP and parked his scooter and having done that, he became aware of the fact that he would not even be able to retrieve it. He planned to finish his job and then take an auto rickshaw to get some cash for retrieval of his scooter, but as he was about to sit in the auto, his elder brother Ramesh, the soberest of the four of them and the only civilian in the family, met him there most unexpectedly and to his great relief.

Bhai Sahib not only got him his scooter back but treated him to a much desired cup of coffee and refreshments. He also gave his younger brother a little extra alongwith the rap he deserved. The rap proved to be futile and that 'little extra' once again got dumped on me.

His belief in the maxim of God looks after fools and infantrymen only got more fortified.

❑

29

Futuristic Planning and Promotion

> *"Smile cannot be bought, begged or borrowed or stolen for it is no earthly good to anyone till given."*
>
> **– Anonymous**

Back after a rather eventful leave, everything was moving at its usual military pace. We had been there in the station for about two years plus and had, therefore, started expecting his posting. During that time, the unit from the field area, from where we had delinked, was moving to a peace station. He came up with the bright idea of despatching our heavy luggage and non-essentials with the unit, so that when we move finally, the journey turns comfortable. I take my share of the responsibility for not having fought the atrocious idea effectively and for having relented to it.

Whatever was thought non-essential including our recently acquired refrigerator were deinducted and we were back to square one. That evening when he returned after despatching the luggage, he was complaining of chest pain. The situation became grim. We were worried and concerned and, without losing any time, reached the MH where some detailed investigations were done and he was found to be in good health. Subsequently, the chest pain was diagnosed to be a natural outcome of 1,000 soldierly hugs he subjected himself to when he met his transiting unit.

We started waiting for his posting. Days turned into weeks and weeks into months but posting did not materialize. Then some rumour started circulating that Lt Col Grewal (of 'Reshma aur Shera' fame), who had taken over a new unit, wanted Vj in his team and we were not to go to the unit/station where we had sent our luggage. It was quite a situation, our bilateral fights became more frequent and more intense. We began planning to retrieve the misdirected luggage. God once again looked after his fool (me) and infantrymen (Vj) and our posting came and to the original unit only but after about a year plus. We hardly had anything and even from whatever little we had the non-essential as he very annoyingly called them were deinducted. How comfortable would have been living with those self-inflicted acute deficiencies can only be imagined and can certainly not be articulated in black and white where you got to stay within the norms of decency.

After an interminable wait, we were finally reunited with our baggage and I was relieved to find it in good shape. The place was Roorkee and Lt Col KS Dyal was in command of the unit. Vj rates him as the best man he ever met and I agree with him, which is very rare. We joined the unit and it was like a home coming. Vj was once again the Adjutant and it was the same team. There were little changes and we took off from where we had left.

It was here that I picked up a good job and my father stopped getting reports of the red entries in our pass book. We then became the proud owner of a Colour TV and were the first in the town to get one and, thus, were natural hosts for most of the major events of Asiad 82.

Among the very few plus points Vj has, is the one of punctuality. He is never late whether it be an official, social or family commitment. At times it becomes agonising but then gradually I too have picked up this trait. That day, it was already 5 O'clock in the evening and there was no trace of his return and, to top it all, I learnt that he was partying in the Officers' Mess. That also happened to be a day when little Pragati was at her prankiest worst. I confess to be at sub-zero level of tolerance when he finally showed up. I let him have it left, right and centre. He sat down in his uniform only and started interacting with his daughter, who had lately acquired a goat and was not finding anything more interesting than her little 'Kajri'. I was getting increasingly impatient and was repeatedly asking him to change his uniform and get into something better to go for some domestic errands to the local market, but he would not budge.

Seeing my volatile mood, he eventually threw in the towel and told his little daughter, who could not indeed understand, that he had got his promotion. The little child did not register it but mercifully I did, but did not know how to congratulate and respond.

❑

30

Staff College Preparations

After living a pretty eventful life, a woman died and was marched in front of 'Account Keeper'. Her sins and pious deeds were discovered to be at the same level, both qualitatively as also quantitatively. It became a difficult decision, whether to send her to heaven or hell. It was then decided that she should be asked a question and if the reply was correct, heaven's gate be opened on her and in case of failure to give the correct answer she be sent to hell. She was ready for the big question and then Chitragupt asked her the spelling of 'Dog', which she correctly answered and was admitted to the paradise. In due course of time, her husband on earth also died and was found to be having a similar score card. Meanwhile, Lord Chitragupt had to go on a TD and he deputed that woman to officiate for him. She told her husband the ground rules in case of a 50:50 score line and asked him to be prepared to answer the spellings. The man was ready for the test and she asked him to spell "Chrysanthemum". Poor chap is still languishing in hell.

Defence Services Staff College (DSSC) is located in Tamil Nadu, in Nilgiri Hills at Wellington and the entrance to it is through an extremely hard entrance examination for which you have to learn all your spellings from 'Dog' to 'Chrysanthemum'. It, therefore, entails very detailed preparations and for that most of the officers utilise all their admissible leave entitlements.

Vj had decided to take this examination and so had Old Jaipal. Both were busy studying and were burning the midnight bulbs, and I think we were rendering them all possible family support in terms of logistics and morale.

On one such evening, which was pretty hot as evenings in Northern Indian Summers can be Good Old Jaipal was all alone at home and was at his desk. By his own admission, he was only attaired in a 'Lungi', and if anybody does not know how to wear a 'Lungi', he is friend Jaipal.

There was a knock at the door and, for some inexplicable reasons, the studious officer thought that it was Vj knocking at the door. From inside only he shouted, *"Han ji – Buha khol daeya ya pehle kurta pa laeya"* – (Yes Sir, should I open the door first or should I wear the shirt). In his illogical obsession, he was thinking that if Vj was alone, he will not mind the door being opened with his uncovered upper, but if I also was accompanying Vj, he will ask him to wear the shirt.

The knock on the door was not by Vj but was, in fact, from the new CO of the unit who had come calling alongwith his wife. Taken aback by the reaction from behind the closed door the CO answered as was demanded, *"Kurta pa lo"* (wear your shirt). Jaipal still did not realise that it was not Vj and replied again, *"Acha ji, fir zara dair"* – (Okay Sir, then wait a little). He then wore his shirt and opened the door, wearing a Lungi reaching just about below the knee level and a shirt unpressed and buttoned. It was certainly not the dress to receive the CO, in fact not even appropriate to receive anyone. CO of course, being a very important man and more so when he was with his wife, who were both immaculately dressed for the evening to call on one of his officers. What subsequently followed once the door was opened is not of consequence, but what followed a few days later is.

The time was past dinner. Vj wanted to have some fresh air and both of us came out for a short walk. We are generally not very bold in dressing and are a bit of conformists, but Jaipal is or at least till then was an incorrigible rebel. Inspite of the aforementioned embarassment, he was again having a walk in almost the same attair, the only change being that this time he was with his wife Raj. Four of us somehow got linked up and were on the main road of the cantonment when the CO's vehicle was seen approaching from the opposite direction. Realising the situation, Jaipal ran and hid behind a dark and big tree. CO spotted the three of us. He stopped there for a while and insisted on us getting in his vehicle for a late night cup of coffee at his residence, which Vj readily and mischievously agreed. Three of us, including Jaipal's wife went away leaving Jaipal clinging to his chosen tree.

❑

31

Mismatch Confirmed

At the time of our marriage, Vj was a Major and had to become a captain when he had his first posting on staff. He once again got his major's rank on posting back to unit. This 'Sine Theta' curve comes in the career of almost all Army Officers and there is nothing unusual about it but to those, who are not well informed, it does not look very complimentary. The difference is of acting and substantive ranks, which is not discernible to civilian society. It is by no means a demotion which it appears to be to the less informed.

Quite a few years after marriage, while doing nothing in Connaught Place, we happened to come across an old colleague of Papa, who knew our family well and had even attended our marriage. The gentleman was visibly disappointed to meet Vj and to see the daughter of his boss married to a worthless man, who was just alternating between the two ranks of Captain and Major. He did convey his feelings indirectly to us and more directly to Papa, who mercifully knew better but could never convince his reluctant subordinate, which perhaps must have been the only time.

A few years later, Vj became a Lt Col and more than anyone else wanted to meet that uncle of mine to correct his impression. But by then, it had become much too late. Death had claimed him and he sadly went away with that impression only.

First impressions are not always the last impressions and are often overshadowed/eclipsed by latest impressions, which may be beyond redemption. Vj is now waiting for the great day of Quayamat or Praley to meet my departed uncle as a brigadier and I wish him all the luck.

❑

32

Abandoned Vehicles of 1971 War

The unit was once again in field area and just across were the enemy lines. Luckily, a river flew between the two adversaries to keep them from accidental or deliberate bravado, but both the sides did have certain enclave across the river, which were dominated by various means including patrolling.

Vj was about to delink and proceed to Wellington for the Staff Course and thus, finally, handed over the job of Adjutant. He was commanding the forward most company and was actually enjoying doing that, having studied enough and successfully for entrance into Defence Services Staff College. He had shifted his concentration to physical fitness and driving. I visited him there and was quite amused and surprised to see the conditions that were there.

There was a herd of animals – cows and pigs. They had been living in the wild ever since '71 and had learnt the safe alignment of the Line of Control. They had come to know the danger that manifested for cows if they strayed into the areas controlled by Pakistanis and the threat to the lives of the pigs, if they moved towards our sides. They, thus, lived, moved and grazed along the no man's land happily as a one big joint family.

The biggest eyesore were, however, a few vehicles abandoned that side of the river by our troops who had to undertake a local withdrawal during '71 war. It had become a famous withdrawal and is now studied in almost all the courses of instructions to draw lessons from it.

Years later, when Vj was doing Senior Command (SC) course at Mhow, the same battle was being presented and studied in great details. At the end of the 'Presentation' during the 'Question Hour', an officer got up and said that during the battle, his unit was there and had to withdraw abandoning a few vehicles across the river and wondered as to what happened to those vehicles. Another officer stood up and said that his unit was there in 1975 and those vehicles were still there and that area had been named as 'Barbad Vehicle Area'. Second Officer got up, whose unit was there in 1979 and confirmed the same status. Yet another confirmation of the same status came from an officer whose unit was deployed there in 1982. The last man up was Vj. He said, "My unit was there in 1984 and those vehicles have been retrieved". That is SIKH LI for you – all the jokes apart.

The retrieved vehicles were shown by Vj to his CO and his Brigade Commander, who expressed their surprise and nothing else. Years later, the retrieved engines were converted to be captive power plants of the unit and subsequently got wasted to Junk Dealers (Kabari).

❑

33

A Blatant Lie

Many including Francis Bacon equate lie as bravery towards God and cowardice towards men and many more equate it as an essential impurity to turn the pure matter into more useful alloy. Nothing of great consequence happened in the Staff College and that one year shot across before we could indeed enjoy it fully well, but nonetheless we did have time of our life.

There is no buddy system in the staff course as is prevalent in many junior level courses like 'Commando' but Vj had found a buddy even in staff course, which is exclusively focused on academics. The two had turned the course into a course for physical fitness. From the top of hill, where our house was located, Vj used to very proudly proclaim that all the roads that were visible from there had been run over by him.

The obsession which he has not been able to outgrow even now when he is well pass 60, often led him to doze off during Central Lectures. He was certainly not the only one to be frequently drifting in slumber, for there were many more with varying reasons.

During one such sleep, he had badly sprained his neck and had to go for some medical attention. The doctor naturally inquired the occurrance details of the sprain and Vj very shamelessly came out with the blatant lie and blamed horse riding for it—one of those rare sports that he has never indulged in, not even at the time of our marriage, not even while climbing mountains whether for official, recreational or religious purposes.

One year went past and we were to move to our new station and there at Wellington, one could sell all the non-essentials of the household, ranging from single drinking glasses to used socks to TV and refrigerator, very few during those days had cars. We also joined in the renovation drive usefully and gainfully getting rid of some of our wasteful collection.

By this time, our little girl had grown to understand that her parents were always telling her to await the next month for getting her childhood requirements and had started reprimanding and warning us against that.

❑

34

Animals/Birds Management

From the cool green climes of Nilgiris, we were deep in hot, dry and yellow deserts. For the company, there was no dearth of snakes, rats, flies and sand, but it was another very cohesive team and we were very willingly accepted and, on our part, we too joined whole heartedly.

That was the time of famous Exercise Brass Tacks/ Operation Trident, which took the men folk away for a considerable period of time, which I had to brave alone with my little daughter. It was a one-room hut called—Tent Replacement Scheme (TRS) which afforded cover only from observation and was open to all other forms of ingress from rats to sand to vagaries of the weather. Electricity came once in a while and primarily we were back to good old hurricane lamps. There were a few more families and together we all formed and even enjoyed a zero option Symbiosis.

Every bad phase like the good one must end and so did that period. The operational disengagement brought the soldiers back and we even got a new accommodation. During this time, an important visitor was to transit through the station and had to spend a night at the place. He was being accompanied by his wife. The Brigade Commander had known the General from an earlier association and wanted to take very good care of his ex boss. Another good thing in the Army is—once a boss, always a boss.

As we all are aware, trees are extremely rare and important in deserts and whatever few are there, are to be shared most cordially among the humans, animals, reptiles and birds. The Guest Room was under one such tree, utilizing its natural canopy to the maximum. While the animals, both domesticated (cows, buffaloes, camels, dogs and pigs) and wild (blue bulls, antelopes, foxes, rats and rabbits) were prevented ingress by barricading the area, the birds had a free flight and access.

The Brigade Commander did not like the idea of birds disturbing his guests early in the morning, particularly after a very hard, short and hectic night. He desired the tree to be 'bird free' for the important morning. A full scale mission was launched. Another tree, where the birds were to be shifted, was identified in the nearest possible vicinity and was made more attractive from bird's eye-viewpoint and, simultaneously, the original abode was made to suffer loss of esteem without, of course, impacting its shade coverage, for that was essential to retain the Guest Room at a comfortable temperature level.

It is no great deal for the Army to create artificial sound effects and shake the branches of the tree to an unhabitable level. It happened for a couple of days and, finally, the birds were happy to migrate to their new home.

The big day arrived, the night came and the guests were conducted to their comfort. It was a nice sleep and no one disturbed, not even birds. The morning happened peacefully and when the guests were being seen off, the General very casually remarked, "Last time, when I passed through and stayed in this very Guest Room, there was very pleasant twitter of the birds, but then the most good things are receding."

❑

35

Hit from Below Poverty Line

"A laugh is worth a hundred groans in the market."

– Charles Lamb

Perhaps Lamb did not appreciate the embarrassment it can cause in a market place, and more so when it targets someone who does not deserve to be its butt.

The market was just about 15 km from our residence and the only way to commute was on our 150 cc two wheelers, negotiating through the sand accumulated on the non-existent roads. Under such circumstances, whenever some officer was going on his 4 × 4 Military Vehicle, we all very readily accompanied. That day it happened to be Vj and all of us ladies accompanied him.

While all of us were doing our shopping, Vj chose to wait for us, sitting in his vehicle only. The military discipline also compelled his driver to move away a little distance. Vj as usual was sitting in the vehicle, either enjoying his music or perhaps some magazine when a beggar woman approached him. She asked for some money, which he never possesses and did not possess at that time, however, he did not feel the necessity to tell the truth to her, and even if he had the chances of her believing him were next to none. He, therefore, rightly told her that he did not have any change. To his surprise, she shot back that she would able to give him the required change. Totally non-plused, he told her that he had only Rs. 100 Note, not expecting her to have such kind of change, but that day, God was too busy looking after the fools and had no time for infantrymen. The beggar woman again surprised him and told him that she would be able to handle that kind of Note too. Eventually, fully cornered, he confessed that he actually did not have any money. As expected, she did not believe him and most arrongantly shouted back at him, "Dusht (Villain), Papi (Sinner) backwas karta hai" (talk non-sense). Having thus rebuked him, she walked away.

Poor man was left morally bruised and looking around and was relieved to notice that no one around was witness to his public humiliation by a begger woman.

❑

36

Man-Animal Bonding

From among the animals, dogs are certainly the most favourite pets. While all other animals domesticated by man give something in return, dogs only give love and loyalty and that is the clinching factor in favour of their ever increasing popularity. It is said that if you pick up a dog from the street and feed it with a bread, it will never bite you and that is the difference between a dog and a man.

In the field area, every post has its own set of stray dogs, which, in fact, cannot be called stray because they so fully belong to that particular post. Men may come and go, units may change but these dogs continue from generations to generations. They are round the clock voluntary sentries and keep the company of the guards. They are generally the first ones to detect an attempted enemy infiltration or penetration and when the real bullets fly, they often lose their life or limb. In return, they are fully adopted by the men on the post and are quite affectionately fed.

The same relationship continues even in peace areas and inspite of there being no operational role for them, every Cook House has its own integral team of dogs, permanently attached to it for ration and shelter. In peace areas, another set of dogs that starts belonging to the unit, are the pet dogs of officers and their families.

Coming down to the incident that I wish to present before you. We were back to the unit and Vj was, as always, tasked to write an important exercise for the unit. He was given the required wherewithall in the Officers' Mess Guest Room and since we had just moved in, we too were staying in the adjacent room. While he was writing the exercise, he was constantly being disturbed by some loud barking and fighting of the dogs. He called his Orderly and asked him to chase away the disturbing lot. The man went out and chased them away but as soon as he returned, the dog fight resumed. This sequence continued for a couple of times. Vj again asked him to do the needful and do it more diligently and effectively. By this time, he too was equally irritated and said, *"Sahib eh civilian kutey han, enhan da discipline bahut kamzor ha"* (Sir these are civilian dogs and their discipline is very weak). These were of course, the dogs that did not belong to the aforementioned categories.

❑

37

The Improved and Preserved Status

After about a year with the unit, Vj got his promotion to the rank of Lt Col and we moved to another field area and once again in the land of rising Sun. The situation there was at its worst and he was straightaway into his usual haunt 'The Operations Room'. He was more there than at home.

That was also the year we bought our first car, a Maruti Omni (Van), which was much in vougue those days. We had gone to collect the vehicle from Guwahati a good about 200 km away and till then, none of us three knew how to drive—today I am the only exception. The car was collected and we requested the Dealer to give us a driver till our lodgings which he very kindly did. Thereafter, well past dinner when Guwahati traffic had thinned down considerably, Vj took out the car to get used to driving, for next day, he was to take it to our place, a distance of 200 km as stated above. I refused to accompany him but our little daughter did and both of them started to move on the city roads which had not yet fully retired for the night. As expected, they caused a traffic jam at the busy cross road junction. A policeman came to book them with a fine but realised that the father-daughter team was in their new car. He confirmed, "Nutan Hai" (Is it new?) and took pity on them. By first light, Vj was an experienced driver and we lost no limbs in our drive back.

Due to operational scenario that prevailed, the city was almost like a fortress after the last light, but that was to our advantage because whatever time he returned from the Operations Room, we could go for a drive—our little share of good time. The little girl almost always was asleep in the car only during our return journey.

During those times only, he managed a few days off and we took off for Shillong, approximately 250 km away, in our new car. The Inspection Bungalow (IB), where we were staying, had only one garage and we were lucky to get it for our car but had we taken the car out of it, surely some other car would have moved in. In the incessant rains of the East, we could not risk this on our new car consequently the whole of Shillong and the adjoining areas were seen either on foot or in hired transport. Little Pragati was extremely annoyed and felt that her complete holiday had been ruined. To date she feels that and chides her father for the most illogical decision.

❑

38

Commonality of Interests

Coincidently, the station was full of Rekha's admirers and she dominated the complete social scene of the cantonment as she did dominate the contemporary Bollywood scenario. In the station there was even a mock queue for registration in the next births for Rekha's affection. It was not only amusing for we ladies but was even irritating at times. One of us even went to the extent of wishing to become Rekha's dog so that none of those men could gain their missed access.

Then one day, Rekha decided to get married with a Gentleman called Mukesh Agarwal, who was the owner of an Electronic Company, which went by the name 'Hot Line'. Total gloom had descended on the mass and monodirectional amorous affairs of the cantonment. All the gilted lovers were into very serious mock mutual consolation and were the butt of ridicule from the ladies, but then that is how we laugh together.

A few days later, I got a telephone call from the Duty Officer, who wanted to know the whereabouts of Vj. Since everyone knew everyone in the station, even the most serious official calls started and ended with social niceties. In fact, irrespective of the situation obtaining this is the norm in the Army circles. I told him that Vj was as usual in the 'Operations Room'. He regretted his non-availability and told me that he wanted to convey a good news. That was also the time Vj was expecting his next rank and the news was to come through the same channel only and any day. I naturally got interested and asked him to share the good news with me if the official confidentiality did not prevent. He very readily and very jubiliently informed me that Rekha's husband had died and the news was on the electronic media. I did not know how to react but did tell him that all of them were being collectively mean. They were, however, neither sorry for Rekha nor for the man. Subsequently, we all learnt that Rekha herself was not indeed sorry for the sad demise. As for the man, the men were overtly jealous for the quality of life he led and were not at all mindful of the small duration of his bliss as they classified it. They even showed envy for the methodology in which the poor man committed suicide. Even Geeta's philosophy was invoked to convey that death is inevitable but what matters is the bigness of life and not its length. A couple of days with Rekha and eventual hanging with her 'Dupatta' were considered to be ultimate that a man could wish for—as per those unilateral amorous patients.

It is most unlikely but should the great thespian ever happen to read these words, I apologise to her for writing this and I apologise on behalf of those actually harmless men who did not mean any ill will to their favourite star, but were having their private little fun and no, not even at anybody's cost, for none was privy to their play acting.

❑

39

The Famous Local Purchase

As expected, the news of Vj's approval to the next rank came before long and we were mentally preparing to leave and again, as was expected, he moved to do another course, 'Senior Command (SC)' at Mhow in the state of Madhya Pradesh (MP). Mhow, near Indore in the Army circle, is known to be Mecca of Infantry, where Infantry officers keep going periodically and quite frequently to do various courses of instructions. Many a times, Mhow is also explained as Military Headquarters of Warfare.

Vj left for the course post-haste and both my daughter and me were left behind. Timing it all with the school vacations of little Pragati, both of us joined him for about three weeks at Mhow. Since it was designed to be a very short stay, we had decided to dine in the Officer's Mess only. There was, thus, lot of time available with me and I had even formed some friendships with the ladies who too were on a short sojourn like me.

Mhow is or at least was famous for dresses available with the adornment of 'smoking' and I alongwith other ladies was generally on a shopping spree. Availability of finances is also not a major restriction in Mhow, for knowing the fiscal health of the Army Officers most of the shopkeepers gladly entertain postdated cheques, without any qualms or discount. There are some local bankers also available, who encash such cheques with affordable commission. With the availability of ATM, Credit/Debit

Cards and All Station Cheques, I am sure Mhow's culture must have been impacted, beyond recognition for folks like us, from earlier generation.

I had collected quite a lot of goodies and a larger lot was in the pipeline with the tailor. Our day of departure was drawing nearer and nearer but the tailor had disappeared. Vj does not take any interest in my such pursuit and thus it was between Pragati and me and, of course the absconding tailor. The tailor's shop luckily was not very far from our apartment and both Pragati and me always kept it under surveillance in turn through Vj's service binoculars which we had learnt to use—necessity is the mother of not only inventions or discoveries, but also of expertise. We were finally successful one day, when my daughter shouted from her 'Observation Post' that the shop was open. Without wasting any time, we rushed to him and retrieved my smoking suits in whatever unfinished or semi-finished state they were, after imposing the appropriate financial rebate. Little Pragati did some excellent running thereafter and informed our co-sufferers about the retrieval opportunity and, thus, also brought herself and her mother some well earned goodwill—yes, the mobile phones had not yet appeared.

❑

40

The Reluctant Eggitarian

I do not know whether the chicken came first or the egg but eggs have troubled me a great deal and I actually wish that they never should have come. Officer's Mess, where we had decided to dine, offered three types of menus: Vegetarian, non-vegetarian and the eggitarian. Vj thought that he did a very smart job by declaring each one of us three in the different category. The aim was to have variety and the best of the menu from across the complete spectrum, particularly, since at the end of it, all of us were to eat together. Theoretically, it was a very practicable idea, but practically, it proved to be exactly the opposite.

In real terms an eggitarian was to have two eggs each for all the three meals and very often on egg-based pudding after the dinner. On an average, it worked out to be almost seven eggs per day. Day after day after day.

When the three menus reached the state of table spread, the father and daughter team almost exclusively concentrated on the vegetarian and non-vegetarian parts and I, who was officially declared an eggitarian, had to sort out or more appropriately get sorted out by eggs, eggs and more eggs. I tried braving it all, but it took better of me and started getting on my nerves, temper and peace, and there was no help forthcoming from any quarters. Vj in the cover of dieting at times left his two breakfast eggs also for the all-devouring egg eater—poor me. The eggs logically started reaching the 'Domestic Helps' and even their families but my later education tells me that such philanthropy is not indeed recognised by the God.

I was, however, certainly not alone in my peculiar predicament. There were quite a few ladies and officers and I suspect even 'Domestic Helps', suffering in silence. Among my co-sufferers was a gentleman by the name Lt. Col. Lui, a burly Zambian, approximately triple my size. One day, he very anguishly and loudly protested, "I cannot have seven eggs a day, day in and day out" and this came as a great relief to me and my eggitarian tribe. We too joined in wholeheartedly and protested that if Lui could not have such an egg onslaught, how could we be expected to sustain it. The point was well received by the Mess Committee and corrective measures were applied. However, by the time everything started falling in place, my time in Mhow was up and I was packing much like a selfless fighter after successfully combating the 'Smoking Tailor', 'The Mess Menu' and, last but not the least, the Father-Daughter Team. I was much too relieved to leave but even that became interestingly hard.

Trying to recover his lost credibility with me, Vj had come to see us off at the Railway Station in Indore. A visit to Indore Bazar was very precisely timed with the start time of our train. We were moving around the Indore Bazar when the little girl felt like having a new pair of shoes. She tried one pair and liked it immediately. She gave her approval and got up to walk with her new shoes only. Seeing her so happy with her new acquisition, Vj refused to ask her to remove them and the illogical fatherly overindulgence cost me most of the contents of my not-so-thick purse. I boarded the train with barely enough to make it to Delhi but thank God for Jaipal and his family and his servant and my own father-in-law were not escorting me. It was more comfortable and we reached Delhi and our house less embarrassed.

❑

41

Identity Annexation

Losing an Identity Document or Identity Card is a Court Martial offence under the Army Act and by the same equation stealing or depriving a person of his Identity should also be an offence under the Army Act, but strangely neither losing nor depriving a person of his actual identity is considered to be under the same gravity, at least as far as I know and as is proved by the under-mentioned episode.

Back from the course and together in Delhi, we ran into another problem. My father-in-law (Bauji) was taken seriously ill and was hospitalized in the MH at Kirby Place (Delhi Cantt). We were staying at Janak Puri. Vj's sister, Baby and Sudhir (Wing Commander Chaitanya of Hyderabad fame) were also in Delhi and were staying at Palam. Most of the times, we used to be moving to or from the MH. Vj had consequently taken Sudhir's scooter and generally either his mother or me were with him on the pillion. The situation, to say the least, was bad solely due to the sickness that was making Bauji suffer, but when we look back, we find moments to laugh together even in those very trying times, and actually this has also been a major lesson in the long journey of life, if it can be imbibed; 'if', because it is not that easy. In the succeeding paras, however, I am going to narrate the lighter side of those grim times.

Vj came out from the MH, that day he was all by himself, he drove to Gopinath Bazar and asked his scooter to be topped up at the Petrol Pump. Having got the petrol he discovered, as usual, that he had no money. Nonetheless, in cantonment, with an Andhra Pradesh Number plate on the scooter and himself looking every inch his own self—a Defence Officer, there was no problem encountered and the Petrol Pump attendant very cordially told him to pay at his convenience. Vj had, however, introduced himself as Wing Commander Chaitanya, living at Air Force Station, Palam, just to assure him of his genuineness. Next day promptly the dues were cleared by me. A few days later, the same sequence got re-enacted but Vj's credibility was well established and no road block was found.

Vj's leave finished and luckily Bauji also recovered *albeit* temporarily and we came back to our Eastern Home. By this time his posting was received and we were once again to watch the sun set and the whole breadth of the country was to be traversed, but before we could actually move, Bauji passed away. The oldest family soldier had departed but this, however, is not the last you hear of him because one of the incidents involving him at his naughtiest best I am saving to be recounted at the end.

Taking a 'U' turn from the unintended emotional digression, I revert to the main tale of the episode. Sudhir and Baby were in Delhi and once they happened to move through Gopinath Bazar on their scooter, and went to the same petrol pump for refuelling. While putting the petrol in the scooter, the attendant could not resist himself and told Wing Commander Chaitanya that he knew that scooter and it was of Wing Commander Chaitanya. Sudhir probably felt important to know that he was so well known. He said, "Yes I am Wing Commander Chaitanya," but the man now gave him a know-all grin and a polite shut up call by saying, "Sir, I even know Wing Commander Chaitanya very well and, of course, you are not him."

❑

42

Minor Adjustments

Naik Natha Singh requested his Company Commander for a casual leave of 10 days. Company Commander, Major Malik was suffering in his own eyes for below par performance while facing the enemy and very desperately wanted an image makeover in his own estimation. He asked old Natha to bring some important article of military value from the enemy side and only then will he get the leave. The old experienced Non-Commissioned Officer (NCO) said, "Right Sir" and went away. Next day, he came to the Major and presented before him an enemy Medium Machine Gun (MMG). The Company Commander was thrilled and asked for one more before the grant of the leave. Next day, another MMG was brought to him. The Company Commander sanctioned the leave but asked Naik Natha Singh as to how he captured the two MMGs without a fight or, in fact, without even a single bullet being fired. Natha dismissed the anxiety very casually and said, "Sir, after all, they (enemy) also have to go on leave."

Once again at close quarters with the enemy, and this time Vj was in command of the unit. Those were very serious and testing times for him. I am privy to some aspects and am not privy to many others. It was certainly a question of survival and safety but he successfully waded through it all—God indeed looked after his infantryman. My own terms of reference do not allow me any foray into the direr aspects of those days and neither am I in the full know-of-it-all and so I take a 'U' turn to be back with the lighter side of soldiering.

He had gone out for an Operational Familiarisation to the forward areas and was to stop for a cup of tea in the evening at one of his Border Out Posts (BOP) which was being held by the Border Security Force (BSF). The BSF Company Commander happened to be an old acquaintance and had extended a kind invitation to me also, to join the CO for a cup of tea.

I reached there at the right time and was 15-20 minutes before the Estimated Time of Arrival (ETA) of the CO and his party. His obsession of punctuality has even rubbed on me too and I never recall being late anywhere, anytime. Awaiting his arrival, I was watching around and the BSF men had kindly given me a pair of binoculars to amuse myself. In turn, they were quite impressed to find me to be quite an expert at its usage. I had the expertise of my 'Tailor Surveillance Days' of Mhow.

In due course, I spotted three vehicles approaching the BOP and instinctively knew those to be that of Vj, but I grew immediately suspicious to see them advancing from a direction. which I thought should not have been friendly. I voiced my concern to the BSF Commander standing nearby and watching the scene from another pair of binoculars. He very consciously pacified me and confirmed to me that it was the CO only. I was still not comfortable with the direction from which the CO was coming and could now see him distinctly across the two Border Pillars (BP). The BOP Commander was again his cool self and told me that he was well aware of the route and the direction and a little bit of give and take in the interests of shortcuts were minor adjustments both the sides permitted and did not mind.

Those minor adjustments were subsequently prohibited by the CO. I am not, however, aware of the present state, specially with barbed wire fencing also having come up.

Our tenure in that area came to an end and we were once again to move Eastwards. East had almost become a second home for us and not only we did not mind being there, we actually enjoyed those environments and the climatic conditions.

This time we were to move in a 'Military Special Train' – an experience in itself, which warrants a separate narration.

❑

43

A Military Special Train : West to East

A Military Special train was moving at its leisurely pace. The Section Commander (A Naik commanding 10 men) was in command of a compartment and two men were duly posted on the gates as sentries. The train came to a halt. The Section Commander relaxing inside with his 2IC inquired from the sentry, *"Oye Mundya Keri Jagah aa Gayi"* (O Youngster, which is the place?). The sentry looked out and spotted a huge Water Tank and started reading C-A-P-A – CAPA, C-I-T-Y – CITY = CAPACITY, and immediately informed the senior man, "Ustad it is Capa City." The Section Commander had no more questions and the train moved on. A few minutes later, the train stopped again and the same question came from inside. The boy looked out and saw another Water Tank and read another CAPA CITY, and shouted back "Ustad, it is CAPA CITY only." The wise man from inside retorted, "You chaps must be careful, CAPA CITY has already been left behind, it has to be CAPA CANTT".

The whole unit of approximately 1,000 men, with their families, well-known to each other, travelling together in the same train over a distance of approximately 2,000 km for a period of seven days with live stocks (goats, sheep and pigs), rations, band, messes, vehicles and all necessary stores is the greatest possible picnic on wheels. The train could be stopped anywhere for any length of time to enjoy the hospitality of various other units located enroute or else to stop, cook, eat/party and move.

Lt Col Jaipal Malik – yes, my famous escort and hero of many other episodes that I have already narrated was now Vj's 2IC. I do not think Vj could get a better 2IC and Vj agrees with me, was in his element. The CO had desired nothing short of the very best Menu for the duration of the journey and the 2IC was most willingly organised to provide. Never have I regretted my Navratra's Vegetarianism so much. The train would be stopped at the station of our choosing on as unfrequented platform, cleaned by the Railways and super cleaned by our own staff. Mats, rugs and carpets were spread, folding chairs laid out, fans, circulators and coolers made functional, music played live and the best of the menu spread. It was a time to bond and enjoy.

The children got around their parents and they, in turn, got around Jaipal. The 2IC, whom everyone knew, will never get a negative from the CO. The train was organised to stop at Ludhiana. Mothers and children went over to the bazar alongwith some uncles who knew the town well and came back with their fancy bicycles and garments.

At another station, pigs of the unit were found to be uncomfortable in their boggy. The train was stopped, an ice factory was got opened and the piggery on wheels was made nice and cool.

Came Roorkee and both the seniormost men, CO and the 2IC wanted to see the plots of land they had bought at that place through Army Welfare Housing Organization (AWHO). The train was stopped for the dinner and while the dinner was being cooked, a couple of Two Wheelers were pulled out for a visit to the AWHO Colony. Mission completed, dinner had and move commenced.

How quickly did those seven days pass! And before long, we were detraining. It was the same Railway Station where about a decade and a half ago, we had detrained with our 'THERMOS BOTTLE'. By this time, we had, of course, learnt that there is something called a "Transfer Voucher", and for three of us, it was a second home coming.

❑

44

A Cycle Expedition

The grim situation that I wrote about in the previous chapters was fully retrieved and everything was looking up, but it had taken better part of three years of total and honest indulgence. What was extremely satisfying was the all-round acknowledgement and, thus, Vj was a contented man, but then Vj's posting to the next station and new appointment was received.

During that stay of more than three years, the boys had been requesting to go to a historical Gurudwara, which was about 200 km from the unit location. Vj was quite liberal with such requests and now when his posting had already been received and unit's move to next station too was anticipated, there was a sudden spurt in the request to go to the Gurudwara. This was also the time when the unit was to celebrate its Raising Day, which is military equivalent of a birthday. It is the day when the unit gets formed and is celebrated very elaborately.

Vj asked in the 'Monthly Unit Sainik Sammelan' as to who all wanted to go to the Gurudwara. Hundred percent hands came up. He told them in that case when everybody wanted to go to Gurudwara, the forthcoming Raising Day would be celebrated there.

The required permission for the unit to move to the Gurudwara on bicycles was obtained and a detailed plan was worked out. Nobody wanted to go on leave and those who had to, regretted it. It was almost hundred percent of the present strength of the unit. Good about 500 cyclists started to be at the holy place, for which they took four days—one way. All of us ladies and families gave them a ceremonial start by peddling with them from the Unit Gates to the end of the cantonment.

Those were also the days when the insurgency situation was quite bad. The cycle column of 500 was led by a truck mounted with an MMG and the second one followed them at the tail, yet another was moving on the flanks of the cycle body up and down. The fourth vehicle was moving on the other flank, playing Punjabi music. Adequate meat was carried in the form of Meat on Hoaf (MOH) and everyday two pegs of rum were authorised to the pedallers.

On the day of arrival in the Gurudwara, it was a pious affair, no meat, no rum and food in the Guru ka Langar. Couple of buses were provided to the ladies and the families and they were timed to be at the holy feet alongwith the cyclists. The Guru ka Langar was also a family reunion. The get together lasted for a few hours and then all of us ladies and families commenced our return journey in our buses. The men started to pedal back and reached the station after four days. It was a novel experience for all of us and was a different way to take leave of the unit and the men you belonged to so wholeheartedly and, thus, Vj ended his regimental, active soldiering days.

❑

45

Narrow Misses

Next two tenures, one after another, were in the dry and hot environs of the Thar desert. Professionally, the time was very satisfying and rewarding for Vj, but during this period, he also had his share of some very close escapes.

Once he just managed to narrowly escape being reduced to two dimensions on the ground by a tank and, in another incident, the trailer, that was attached to his vehicle, decided to overtake the vehicle. On both the occasions, his luck held on and, as they say, a commander should not only be professionally competent but must also be lucky. I am not too sure about the first attribute, but the second one he had in good quantity. The following incident, like many described earlier, proves what I feel.

They were out on 'Operation Vijay', deep in the hot deserts. The formation was being visited very regularly by senior officers and some very senior civilian dignitaries. On one such day, when the seniormost dignitary was to visit a particular spot at night, perhaps for the only time in his career, he cleanly forgot to pass instructions for the activation of the helidrome. By the time the omission was realised, it was much too late and any knee jerk fire fight would have further complicated the situation.

He was, however, very well placed and established with his Boss and the formation. He did whatever could be done to retrieve the situation and then walked upto his Boss to apprise him of it all. Another very fine gentleman and together both of them decided to wait and watch.

At the appointed time, the helicopters reached the visiting dignitaries and sequentially took off to fly them to the intended spot. Those were good about three to four helicopters and the flight time was just about 20 minutes. When the leading helicopter was about to reach the landing helidrome, it was discovered to be unfit for landing due to a local sandstorm and high velocity whirlwinds. The visit had to be called off and the complete entourage returned. This, however, does not impact the operations/exercises programmed on ground which proceed as planned.

Once again, Vj went to his Boss and gave him the latest information and, in his characteristic style, added, "Sir, do not I always say God looks after fools and infantrymen?" His Boss, an equally witty and fine gentleman, shot back, *"Infantryman te to ho gaya, te main ki hoya?"* (Infantryman, of course, are you, but then what am I?) He was from Engineers and rose to be the Engineer-in-chief (Lt. Gen. Ranjit Singh).

❑

46

Disciplining the Wild

I know of an Old Timer, a Colonel, who would stop his vehicle at the traffic signal in the dead of the night, when there would not be a single person moving on the road and that testifies discipline, when right things are done at the right place and time without any external pressure. I have also seen animals, both wild and domesticated disciplined to perfection and do, thus, totally agree with the Late Field Marshal, Sam Manekshaw, who in an interview on television, said that there are only four things lacking in India, namely, discipline, character, leadership and integrity and that there were no other shortages that cannot be tackled.

Coming back to my main course, Vj was now a Brigade Commander with much larger responsibilities and also wore the hat of the Station Commander. I am not too sure if he had a worthwhile head in any of the two hats, but both his seniors and juniors surprised me by thinking so. The station he commanded had two brigades and was almost a model township more like a huge joint family.

During that time, I was once returning from a local market and my elder sister, Neelam was also with me, who had come visiting for some time. Suddenly, the car decided to delink one of its front wheels and I actually saw it flying at a tangent. Luckily, the sand deposit to the road provided us with a soft landing. The officer responsible for the upkeep of the vehicle fleet was understandably quite perturbed. Vj rebuked the young man by saying that if he wanted to do such a good favour to the Commander, he should have been more elaborate in planning and execution.

This was also a station with considerable wildlife. There were herds of blue bulls, deers, foxes and rabbits. They invariably entered the station from all over and nothwithstanding the frequent repair, kept breaking the perimeter wall. Apparently, an atrocious idea struck the Commander, but who could tell him that? During the next repair of the wall, he ordered two gates to be properly erected and even had them sign posted as 'Blue Bull Entrace'. The indisciplined and very muscular animals continued their wayward conduct for a few more days, perhaps for a couple of weeks, but eventually they fell in line and began to respect their stipulated entrance and exit and spared the frequent repair of the wall.

Indiciplined human behaviour is, therefore, totally unacceptable and can actually be eradicated if the will exists.

❑

47

The Local Knowledge

Vj's next posting was from the land of Blue Bulls to Black Cats. He was DIG (Ops and Trg), National Security Guards. The very nature of the job required him to move around the whole country and, at times, even abroad. Sometimes, such visits in the manageable radius were also undertaken by road, and, rarely though, at times in our car. During those very rare sojourns, I also, at times, accompanied him.

It was one such visit and we were passing through the state of Punjab. Whatever job he had to do had already been addressed and we were on our return journey. As often happens, during such drives, we halted for a breather at a roadside Dhaba. The Indian society does not need any introduction to Dhabas but to the negligible minority, I can say that these Dhabas are an inescapable part of Indian Highways and can be vaguely compared to good old motels, with better and fresh food and overwhelming and simple hospitality by sons/daughters of the soil.

Having had a good lunch with chicken (which one selects in live form and is subsequently cooked) and paranthas. I wanted to have a soft drink while my more rural companion opted for Lassi (Butter Milk). I called our all-in-all host, an extremely friendly and enthusiastic youngman and requested him to give me a cold soft drink. He looked at me and in no uncertain manner dismissed my request as an unearthly demand, saying that no such thing existed with him. I found the reply rather insolent, particularly when I could see crates of soft drinks lying around and even a refrigerator functioning. I expressed my surprise but my host was sure and told me that he did not serve drinks. I gave up and convinced myself that perhaps he had exhausted his stocks.

My all-knowing companion was listening to my interaction and was saddistically enjoying his Lassi and my rebuff as he usually does, or should I say as we mutually do. He eventually and uncharacteristically decided to help me out. He came up close and told me that the very question was wrong, so how could I hope to get the right response? I did not understand his comment and dismissed it with disdain and started getting ready to leave. At the same time, I was badly annoyed to see his driver sipping at a Coke.

He called the same boy back and asked him, as only he can, "*Oye kaka, tera kol kariyan, kariyan, pepsian han*" (O young man, which all pepsis you have?). Pat came the reply "*Sir Sariyan hi han*—Coca Cola, Fanta, Limca, *jeri chahidi*" (Sir, I have all the pepsis like Coca Cola, Fanta and Limca, whichever you wish to have).

I did have my soft drink but not without a long moral lecture from him about knowing what to ask where.

❑

48

Magnetism of Yesteryears

Almost three-and-a-half decades in uniform had gone past. Vj had superannuated but almost immediately was employed by the State Government of Jharkhand as Director of Welfare for over 22,000 of Ex-servicemen (ESM) and their families in the state.

Next four years were at Ranchi and retirement turned out to be yet another posting, for the new appointment was taken up within a week of delinking from the NSG. Ranchi tenure, thus, turned out to be the longest as also very satisfying. Vj was tasked to raise the organization from, if I may use a nuclear terminology, ground zero and he left it well established in a healthy operational state and ticking, in full military shipshapeness.

In the state of Jharkhand, there were 100 ESM from World War 2 (WW2). They fought for British Army but had been disowned after usage by Great Britain and understandably they could not have been owned by the Government of India. Consequently, these old men, all in their advanced 80s, were living in abject poverty, neglect and vulnerable health state. Vj was luckily the medium through whom they started getting a monthly pension of Rs. 2,000/-, which for them was a considerable sum from the State Government. My latest information is that this has been raised considerably.

All these men in their frail health would converge on to the state capital, Ranchi from the remotest corners of the state, every month in the first week to collect their pension. They used to spend a couple of days at Ranchi, where free lodging and boarding was extended to them and they would go back happy and rejuvenated.

Concerned with the monthly bother, they had to undertake all the way from their distant villages, not too well connected with the state capital. Vj's Assistant Director, Lt Col AP Singh, another very committed soldier, used to organise in tandem with various banks to have the money delivered to them at their place of residence or as near to it as possible, depending upon the various branches that the banks had functional in the state. The consent of the old men had to be taken for the arrangements to commence but all of them collectively surprised Vj and his Assistant Director. For them, the status quo was a 'monthly picnic' as they called it, where their young sons/daughters/grandchildren willingly brought them. The arrangement impressed upon their next generation and village neighbours that they were still important enough to be hosted by the organization free of any charges. Every month they would meet their old colleagues and talked about the yesteryears spent together in the jungles of Burma, either being chased by the enemy (Japan) or in hot pursuit of the same enemy. Social interaction with old friends had better magnetism than the convenience of getting the pension at the doorstep. The arrangements being thought were dropped and a little extra care was taken to make their monthly stay better.

❑

49

The Low Flight

An woman made worse mistake than mine and married an Air Force Officer. One fine day, when he was trying to reach new heights in the sky, in whatever model of the MIG he flew, he fell down. The lady organised befitting last rites for the departed soul, and when she was returning after the cremation, the Met conditions grew very violent and noisy. Thunderstorm, heavy rains and lightening. She looked up and said, "It appears he has finally reached."

A similar blunder was made by Vj's bhabi, who married his elder brother Raj, with another Air Force Officer. The incident relates to the time they were recently married. He perhaps was also in a great hurry to marry, for he was only a Pilot Officer on the very first posting after being commissioned.

He was posted at Ambala, precisely 205 km from Delhi. Most of these four brothers remained very integral to their parents as long as the older couple was alive, and so was he. Almost every weekend, he would drive those 205 km on his scooter alongwith his wife and be with his family in Delhi to get back to work again on Monday. I do not visualise any objections would have come from anywhere or anyone and the routine continued for quite some time with fresh and better timings recorded in speed every time/weekend.

That day, the young recently married couple was on their Saturday move from Ambala to Delhi. The young man was more famous for low flying rather than driving and had the dubious history of having thrown everyone off the pillion at least once, except Vj, who had the record of tasting the black tarmac twice. Well, back to the famous journey again. Somewhere near Panipat, the young man realised that he had been only making soliloquies without any response from the rear. He looked behind to find that he was the only occupant of the great vehicle without any rear guard. Reckless driving notwithstanding Bhai Sahib is otherwise a very gentle and noble soul.

The TINA (There is no alternative) factor came into being and he started driving back, hoping for the best, and probably fearing the worst. He eventually discovered his newly wed wife in Karnal Hospital bandaged and plastered all over with a fractured leg. The brave girl, after being ejected from the pillion, had somehow reached the hospital at her own and got the required medical attention.

That was certainly not the end of the journey. Having been reunited at the Civil Hospital, the tough couple was back again on the scooter and off to complete the aborted journey. Needless to say, two days later, while the brave driver was back to work, the wounded partner warranted some elaborate and extended nursing in Delhi before being battle worthy.

Years later, both Vj and me were on the scooter at Roorkee. Generally, while driving, Vj is invariably trying to beat both Mohammad Rafi and Kishore Kumar put together and somewhere within does entertain that lop-sided notion. I was and I continue to be the only listener. That day, of course, was special, two singing wasps chose to convert the song into a chorus and went right into the singing source – his mouth. May be one went in and other was content being outside only but the result was immediately manifested. Unlike his Bhabi, he was luckily on the gate of the MH, unlike the poor lady, he was not alone and while she was broken beyond recognition, he was swollen much beyond it and unlike her, his looks generated a lot of laugh, in spite of the pain he suffered.

❑

50

A Ghastly Orchestra

"As you sow, so shall you reap", "tit for tat" or the widely believed theory of Karma gets proved beyond doubt by the episode I am going to place before you, which should more appropriately be termed as a mishap. It occurred in continuation with WW2, which had just ended.

Some of the units of what was till then the British Indian Army were on rest and recoupe. The men and officer alike had let their hair down for it had been a very long and bloody engagement of almost six years. This particular unit or installation or whatever it was then, called was back after the famous, 'Defeat into Victory' of Burma, or Myanmar as it is called now.

My father-in-law, Bauji was part of this unit and it was located somewhere in what is now Pakistan. The partition was good about two years in the realm of future just like the independence. On the edge of the cantonment, and perhaps within it was a Cremation Ground, which was manned by one man, a 'Solitary Reaper'—an Acharya ji—a brahmin, who attended all the last rites and lived all by himself in that total tranquility. Those were also the days when ghosts and witches were still active and were integral albeit scary part of life. Almost everyone had seen them and believed in their existence. Acharya ji's name was Hukma and was respectfully called 'Bhaiya Hukma'. He was held in great awe for his brave, self-imposed, isolated living. He also enjoyed the reputation that had come to surround him and was very selectively interactive with the general society.

One day a group of four to five (G5) soldiers including Bauji decided to rupture Bhaiya Hukma's fearless reputation. The unsuspecting Hukma generally wore one single cloak, somewhat like a dated version of Kaftan, from top to bottom, which perhaps went well with his evocation. The 'G5' one night well past the civil hours collected whatever musical instruments they could find from the temple, Gurudwara or Unit Band and infiltrated into the cremation ground.

Having finished his daily chores, Bhaiya Hukma had retired for the day and was into deep slumber when 'G5' positioned themselves a few meters away from his humble lodging and started playing—actually they could not be playing—they started sounding their musical instruments in the most non-musical manner, as loud as they could in total disharmony and accompanied it all with weirdest sounds created from their lungs, throats and mouths. The total accoustic impact would have woken up all the ghosts, witches and corpses but luckily all of them on that day had perhaps taken a little more than their capacity and kept themselves away from the scene so fearfully unfolding. But old Bhaiya Hukma was a teetotaller and could not continue in his sleep. He grew apprehensive and must even have felt the fear factor encroach upon his cool composure so deliberately built and nurtured. He ultimately decided to brave it all and came out shouting as to who the hell they were. It was all progressing as per the script for 'G5'. Poor Bhaiya Hukma was standing tall, all alone in his trade mark cloak, confronting the five dancing, shrieking and shouting ghosts, when one of them, Bauji, being the shortest of them all, shrieked the loudest and rushed at the man in that cloak. He lifted his cloak and went inside it. He had certainly not gone there on permanent posting and, within a second, escaped out in the opposite direction, but before the escape, could be registered the Oldman had fallen flat on his back and had passed beyond senses, luckily not passed away.

Next day, it was the talk of the town and old Bhaiya Hukma had barely survived the trauma.

Many years later in Delhi, when the colony of RK Puram had just witnessed its first set of inhabitants move in and Army had been allocated sector 2, Bauji and our mother were out for an after dinner walk and coincidently behind them at a distance of approximately 50 meters was Vj's elder brother and bhabi (the Air Force couple). While the junior couple could see their parents walking ahead, the seniors were not aware as to who was coming behind them. Fifty years ago, RK Puram was nowhere as busy as it is now. The colonies of Safdarjung Enclave and Tennis Courts were not even in thoughts till then and the place at night was quite deserted and quiet.

Suddenly, something happened to Bhai Sahib, for it cannot be explained with any logic and he rushed like Bauji had to Bhaiya Hukma and shrieking loudly, passed through between his parents. Bauji's response was identical to that of his target of 30 year ago. He fell flat and had a total blackout. He was badly traumatized and it took quite some time and efforts for the three of them from the family to retrieve him. Bhai Sahib was entitled to all the dressing down he subsequently received and for Bauji, the lesson learnt was as you sow, so shall you reap.

❑

51

The Parting Salute

In these essays and through these pages, I have attempted to encapsule both a grand stand as also a close quarter view of the Army life. The journey has covered major part of my life, from a girl in her 20s to a grandmother in her 50s. The zeal has been honest and no satire or irony has been deliberately attempted. No one has been ridiculed and no sarcasm has been allowed to seap in the narration. However, human frailities and my own inadequacies might have polluted my ink somewhere, for which I am blameworthy and request your magnanimity to be absolved.

Exaggeration is integral to any recapitulation, particularly if articulation is with a view to communicate and more so if it is targetted to facilitate a smile or a laugh and may, therefore, be kindly taken in that spirit.

Thank you for your indulgence.

❑❑❑